"THIS IS A HOLD UP!"

"Inside," Chapman ordered viciously. "We don't want any nonsense."

He pulled out the wheat sack. "Put all the money into that. I'll give you—thirty seconds!"

The cashier went into the vault. In his trembling hands he brought out stacks of money.

Chapman glanced back at the lookout.

"Jim!" cried Clem Tancred.

There were two explosions—one was a gun in the palsied hand of the cashier and the other was Clem's. As Chapman whirled, the cashier was crumpling to the floor.

"I had to do it," Clem said.

THERE WAS NO GOING BACK NOW.

Bantam Books by Frank Gruber
Ask your bookseller for the books you have missed

THE CURLY WOLF
THIS GUN IS STILL
OUTLAW
WANTED!

OUTLAW
FRANK GRUBER

BANTAM BOOKS · LONDON · TORONTO · NEW YORK

OUTLAW

A Bantam Book | March 1959
2nd printing .... March 1963   3rd printing .. February 1980

ISBN 0–553–10727–5

Published simultaneously in the United States and Canada

Bantam Books are published by Bantam Books, Inc. Its trade-
mark, consisting of the words "Bantam Books" and the por-
trayal of a bantam, is Registered in U.S. Patent and Trademark
Office and in other countries. Marca Registrada. Bantam
Books, Inc., 666 Fifth Avenue, New York, New York 10019.

COVER PRINTED IN THE UNITED STATES OF AMERICA
TEXT PRINTED IN CANADA

OUTLAW

One

IN THE FRONT of the coach a half-dozen men were playing poker. The conductor had remonstrated with them before the train reached Lexington, but they had intimidated him with verbal abuse so that he did not come back into this car until the train had stopped at Lexington and gone on again. Some passengers had got on and the conductor was, by necessity of his job, compelled to come through the car and collect the tickets.

He found that the poker game had spread from the two seats into the aisle and that flat bottles were now being openly passed around the group. Furthermore, the bottles had been passed around for some time, for the gamblers had become boisterous.

Tight-lipped, the conductor tried to squeeze past one of the players who was crouched on his haunches in the aisle. The man turned on him savagely. "Who you pushing, you goddam sour-face?"

"I didn't mean to push you," the conductor said in a low tone. "But I must get through. You're—you're blocking the aisle."

The card player caught hold of one of his companions and pulled himself to his feet. "What if I am, you stinking—!"

In a near-by seat, a spinsterish woman exclaimed, "Conductor, I won't stand for such language. I demand that you put that man off this train. And that you stop that gambling. If you don't, I'll report you to your superiors."

The abusive passenger turned drunkenly and searched for the complainant. His eyes came to rest upon a girl in her late teens, who sat in the seat directly behind the one in which the card game was going on. His scowl left his face and he leered drunkenly: "Well, my pretty, so *you* want me run off the train, huh? Is that being sociable to a neighbor, I ask you?"

The girl looked out of the window.

One of the other players said peevishly, "Come on, Pike, if you're going to play, let's play. . . ."

The conductor tried again to pass Pike. The big ruffian

1

pushed him back, absent-mindedly. His eyes on the girl who
was staring out of the window, he lurched forward.

"I was talking to you, pretty face. Why don't you answer
me?"

Halfway down the car, Jim Chapman got up. Pale, partly
from his long siege of illness and partly from cold anger, he
looked even younger than his twenty years. His boots clicked
on the wooden floor of the car as he walked forward.

When he was six feet from the ruffian, Pike, he said, "Get
out of this car, you drunken loafer!"

For a second the words made no impression on Pike, for
he had not expected to be challenged by anyone in the train
after his easy intimidation of the conductor. But then his eyes
popped wide and his mouth opened and showed blackened,
tobacco-stained teeth.

"What was that?" he exclaimed. "Was you talkin' to *me*,
you young pup?"

Chapman took a step forward, raised his right foot and
planted it in Pike's stomach. It was a shove, rather than a
kick, but it was a hard shove.

Pike went back. The conductor, trying to get out of the
way, tripped and hit the floor on his back. Pike stumbled over
him and went down on top of him.

He began cursing luridly. The other card players yelled
excitedly and began squirming and shoving in their cramped
quarters. Pike got around on his hands and knees and looked
up at the youth who had kicked him down.

"You—!" he began and then stopped.

The Navy Colt in Chapman's hand was partly depressed
to cover Pike, but it could easily be swung up and sidewards
should any of Pike's card-playing companions take up the
challenge.

The conductor got to his feet behind Pike. Chapman said
to him, "Stop the train."

White-faced, the conductor reached up and pulled the
signal cord. The sudden braking of the train threw the different card players against one another. Pike went back on his
haunches.

Chapman, braced for the sudden stop, remained in easy
control. "All right," he said crisply. "Get off the train now.
You, Pike, and all the rest of you."

"Hey!" blustered one of the other card players. "I wasn't
doin' nothin'. You can't make me get—"

The Navy Colt swung to the right. "I said, get off."

There was no further argument. The several card players

departed hurriedly from the train. They even left their cards behind. Chapman nodded to the conductor who gave the signal cord two quick jerks and, as the wheels started to turn again, he flicked back the tail of his sackcloth coat and slipped the Navy Colt into a holster, fastened to a belt buckled high about his waist.

Then he walked back to his seat. He did not look at the girl who had been accosted by Pike.

In the back of the car several passengers began talking about the incident. The conductor, his poise somewhat recovered, walked with his swinging gait back to where Chapman was staring moodily out of the window at the passing landscape.

"Mister," he said, "I'm mighty grateful for what you did. That Pike fellow is a bad one. He's traveled with me before and he's always made trouble."

Chapman turned briefly from the window. "It's all right," he said shortly.

The conductor frowned at the rebuff, then shrugged and continued down the train. A heavy-set man in his early forties came forward and sat down beside Chapman.

"That was good work, Stranger," he said. "Took nerve."

Chapman did not even turn from staring out of the window. He began to regret having interfered. The heavy-set man cleared his throat and took an engraved card from the pocket of a brocaded vest.

"Allow me to introduce myself. I am Alan Vickers."

Chapman turned and took the card from his seatmate. He looked at it and read:

VICKERS INTERNATIONAL DETECTIVE AGENCY

Chicago   New York   London

Alan Vickers

Chapman's fingers caressed the card. He looked thoughtfully at Alan Vickers. "How do you do, sir," he said finally.

Vickers inhaled heavily. "You've heard of our firm. I don't mind telling you that I'm on my way to Kansas City where we're opening a new branch office. . . . Do you live out this way, sir?"

Chapman nodded. "Yes. That is, well, I used to live around here. Guess I will again. I haven't been around for some time."

"Ah! A soldier, eh? Let me see, I imagine you've been ill. In a hospital. I'm sorry to hear that. You must have had quite a siege."

"It wasn't so bad," Chapman replied.

No, the hospital hadn't been so bad. He'd only been there two months. It was the long convalescence that had worn him down. The wound had not healed. It still hurt him now when the weather was damp.

"As I was saying, sir," Alan Vickers continued, "I'm opening a branch in Kansas City. I don't mind saying that I was impressed by your performance of a few minutes ago and I was wondering. . . . Well, I'm a man of quick judgment. Would you be interested in going to work for me? At our new branch."

Chapman blinked. "You mean . . . become a detective?"

"Yes, of course. You're younger than most of our operators, but age and experience isn't everything. Much depends on the man himself. Your performance. . . . Well, sir, I like you. I think you'd make an excellent detective. What do you say?"

Chapman turned his face toward Alan Vickers and stared at him. "But you don't know anything about me. You haven't even—I mean, I haven't even told you my name." He paused a moment. "It's Jim Chapman."

Alan Vickers held out a thick, muscular hand. "Glad to make your acquaintance, Chapman."

Chapman took the detective's hand briefly, then released it and leaned away. "I wasn't a Union soldier, Mr. Vickers," he said.

Vickers seemed a little disconcerted for a moment. He coughed once or twice. "Why, ah, the war's over. And after all, we *are* opening this branch in a more or less Southern community. I don't think that should make any difference, Chapman. Might be an excellent idea, in fact, to have a man with the old Southern viewpoint, you might say. But don't give me your answer now. Think it over. Then if you decide that you'd like to try it—come over and see me in Kansas City. I'll be there for two weeks."

Chapman nodded slowly. The conductor came through the car from the rear, calling, "Independence, next stop."

"I'll think it over, Mr. Vickers," Chapman said. He got up and reached to the rack overhead for a rather worn carpetbag. "I'm glad to have made your acquaintance. I get off here."

Vickers got up to let Chapman out into the aisle. He shook hands again. "I'll look forward to seeing you in Kansas City, then."

The train was slackening speed for the Independence station. Ahead, passengers were getting ready to leave. As Chapman passed the girl for whom he had interceded, she suddenly turned and said in a voice only loud enough for him:

"Thank you."

Chapman turned briefly, bowed in acknowledgment and pushed ahead. The girl was getting off, too.

Two

INDEPENDENCE HAD grown. Captured by Price in '61, purged by Jennison and garrisoned by Union and Confederate in turn, the town had nevertheless swelled tremendously. Here and there blackened rubble that had once been houses still dotted the streets, but on the whole, the town showed few scars. Most of the buildings were new, built of lumber and painted.

There were still plenty of blue uniforms on the street, for the town was headquarters for the provost marshal of the district.

Horses lined the hitchrail on the main thoroughfare. Farm wagons were scattered along the street, and men and women walked the wooden sidewalks, going from store to store or standing in small groups, talking.

Chapman walked slowly along the street until he came to the Hoffman House, before which stood a stage that seemed about ready to depart. He picked out a man he judged to be the driver.

"Can you tell me if there's a stage soon for Freedom?"

"You bet," said the man. "This is her. And she leaves right smart now. Just waitin' for folks from the train. Cost you fifty cents. Let me stick your carpetbag in the boot."

Chapman surrendered his bag, paid the driver a half dollar and climbed into the Butterfield coach. There were two men already inside, one a farmer judging by his rough butternut suit and the other a businessman, or perhaps a commercial traveler.

After Chapman had been seated the driver opened the door again on Chapman's side. "Watch your step, Miss," he said. "We're off in a minute."

The girl from the train climbed into the coach and sat down directly opposite Chapman. The man he had taken for a commercial traveler exclaimed, "Why, Miss Comstock! Back from St. Louis already?"

"Yes," replied the girl. "How do you do, Mr. Slocum?"

"Just fine, Miss Evelyn, just fine. Saw your father yesterday. He didn't say anything about your coming back."

6

"He doesn't know I'm coming. I'm surprising him."

Overhead, the stage driver was shouting to his horses. He cracked his whip and the stagecoach began to move. Almost immediately one of the wheels struck a hole in the street and Evelyn Comstock lurched forward in her seat. Chapman's hand went out instinctively to steady her, but she did not lose her balance.

For an instant her eyes met his. There was a quizzical expression in them—almost a question. He turned his face to look out of the window at the store fronts flashing by.

Slocum began talking to the girl about her father. Then, suddenly, the man in butternut exclaimed, "Say, ain't you the Chapman boy?"

Jim Chapman twitched. Beside him he felt Slocum move.

Chapman looked at the farmer and lifted his hands in an unobtrusive gesture. "Yes," he said, "I'm Jim Chapman."

"I thought so!" exclaimed the farmer triumphantly. "You was on'y a boy the last time I saw you, but you're a dead ringer for your older brother Tom; him that was—" he coughed suddenly.

The man beside Chapman said. "Jim Chapman," he said. "Yes, I remember you, too. Didn't you go down to Mexico at the close of the war?"

The farmer across from Slocum was suddenly making signals to the man beside Chapman. Chapman intercepted them and his nostrils flared a little.

"Yes, I went down to Mexico with Shelby. Yes, I rode with Anderson. And my brother was killed at Lone Jack, when he was with Quantrell. And . . . the war's over. Or isn't it?"

"Sure, sure. Certainly," Henry Slocum assured Chapman. "Sorry, didn't mean anything out of the way."

Chapman knew that the girl's eyes were on him, but he stared stonily out of the window. He saw the countryside passing by, heard the driver yelling at his horses. And he was fully aware that he had killed whatever further conversation might have gone on during the nine-mile trip to Freedom. No one inside the coach spoke another word.

When it finally pulled up beside the Freedom Hotel Chapman was the first one out. He got his own carpetbag from the boot and turned away, without further glance at any of his erstwhile traveling companions.

Freedom had changed, too. The square that had seen both the blue and the gray now had a small howitzer planted in the center with a stack of cannon balls beside it. The local com-

pany—the local company of Union men—had taken it at
Vicksburg.

Freedom was smaller than Independence. But it boasted a
college, on the hill at the north edge of town. It was late
afternoon when Chapman swung up the road, and students
were coming from their classes. Some of them were as old
as Chapman, some older. They had taken time out from their
studies to win—and lose—a war. Now some of them were
classmates, some who had faced each other on the battlefields.

A man came out of a house, started to pass Chapman, then
stopped and exclaimed unbelievingly, "Jim Chapman!"

"Hello, Lon," Chapman said carelessly as if he had just
seen Lon Rader the day before. He continued in his stride,
leaving the other staring after him.

Passing the college on the hill, he turned and looked down
on Freedom. His forehead creased for a moment and his
mouth twisted crookedly. Then he turned and looked ahead,
down the dusty road to the north.

He had ridden up this hill four years ago, in September of
'63. Sixteen he had been and he was going to war. War as it
was fought in Missouri. The charge at dawn, the quick thrust
in the night, the yelling and screaming of the men about him,
the terrible staccato of the Navy Colt, the bark and whine of
the Sharp's rifle.

War. Skulking and sniping, flight and pursuit. The torch
and the revolver. Guerrilla warfare. No quarter given and
none expected. The black flag in Lawrence, pillars of smoke
and the blood running in the streets.

It was over now. They had lost and they had paid for it.
Appomattox was two years back and Jim Chapman was just
coming home. There had been too much to forget quickly.
Perhaps they still remembered.

A mile from Freedom he saw the gutted remains of what
had been Abe Colton's fine brick house. Near by was a log
cabin, with gray mud filling the chinks between the logs. A
bearded, one-armed man peered out of the door of the cabin,
drew in his head, then popped it out again. He stared at
Chapman and finally spoke.

"Good lord! . . . Jim Chapman." He came hesitatingly to
the road, but he could not hold out his hand in greeting, because he had no right hand.

Chapman said, "Hello, Abe." He looked past Colton at the
ruins of Colton's house and he looked where Colton's strong
right arm had been.

"We heard you was killed in Mexico," Colton said. "Your sister, Annie . . ."

"My sister?" Chapman said, with quickening tone. "She's . . "

"Oh, no, she's fine. Ed, too. I was just going to say I was talking to her not so long ago and she hadn't heard from you. *She* never said you were dead. Always claimed you'd come back someday, when it was—when things was different."

"And are they different, Abe?"

The bitterness came to Abe Colton's eyes. The bitterness of his ruined home, his lost arm . . . the thwarted years ahead of him.

"It's hell, Jim. Sometimes I think it ain't worth goin' on. If it weren't for the kids . . ." He averted his eyes for a moment, then laughed. "But you'll be wanting to go home, Jim."

"Yes," said Chapman. "Yes, I guess so."

Beyond Colton's the road turned to the east and ran for a winding mile through scraggly forest. Then there was a break in which stood a two-story frame house that had survived the war years. Across the road and a hundred yards farther ahead was Simon Rains' farm, a log cabin and four or five acres of cleared land. Another half mile of woods then and Jasper Hobson's farm was on the right, a recently painted white frame house, to which rooms had been added from time to time so that the house was of a peculiar shape.

Directly across the road, a lane turned off and wound for almost a quarter mile in, to a little clearing, with a knoll in the center of it. On the knoll was a weathered, unpainted frame house of two rooms and attic.

From the edge of the lane, Chapman regarded the house. He put down his carpetbag.

The front door of the house was open and smoke came thinly from the chimney. A few chickens scratched in the dirt to the side and, to the left a little way, a four-year-old boy was playing with a very young, spotted puppy.

Chapman had never seen the child.

"So this is it," he said, half-aloud and, as if to retort to his comment, a woman came to the door. She saw Jim Chapman fifty feet away and stiffened. Although not in recognition. Just in surprise at seeing a stranger so close.

Leaving his carpetbag on the grass, Chapman swung toward the house. Anne would now be twenty-two. She looked thirty. She had borne a child through the black days of Order Number 11. Ed, her husband had been with Hood in Tennessee.

"Hello," Chapman said, as he walked toward the house. "Hello, Annie. . . ."

"Oh, my God," whispered the woman in the doorway, "it's —it's Jimmie. . . ."

He stopped a few feet from the door and looked awkwardly at his sister. They had always been very much attached to one another. Tom and Annie and he. But that had been years ago. Tom was dead now. And Jim had been away for four years.

Anne said, "Jim, I don't—" and then she stepped down from the door stoop and came and put her arms about him. He held her and felt her body tremble. To break the awkwardness of the moment, he twisted his head and said, "Don't tell me that shaver there is my nephew! . . ." He still didn't feel easy with her. He smiled.

She pushed away from him, dabbed at her eyes and smiled through tears. "Tommy!" she cried. "Tommy, come and meet your Uncle Jim."

Tommy left his puppy and came forward, walking with childish dignity. He put both hands in his overall pockets, took them out and wiped them along his thighs, then gravely held out the right hand.

"Hello, Uncle Jim," he said.

Chapman stooped and caught up the boy and tossed him high in the air. He caught him and laughed brittlely. "So you're Thomas Taylor, Jr."

Anne Chapman Taylor ran to the edge of the house, put her hands to her mouth and called: "Ed! Ed—come to the house. Jim's home. Jim, my brother!"

Ed Taylor, unshaven and perspiring from his ploughing, came around the corner of the house. "Jim," he said, "it's good to see you. Annie always said you'd show up some fine day."

Chapman shook his brother-in-law's hand and pounded him on the back. Tom Taylor yelled in glee.

"I'm glad to be here, Ed," Chapman said. "I didn't know I was so homesick until I stood out there a few minutes ago and looked at this old shack. . . . You're looking well, Ed."

"Oh, I'm all right, Jim. A touch of malaria now and then, but I can't complain. I came through in fine shape."

"My daddy was a sergeant," piped up Ed Taylor's young son, "and he could lick any two Yankees in the army. He could even lick General Sherman, he could."

Ed Taylor smiled at his son. Then he said, "Annie, Jim probably hasn't eaten."

"Of course!" Chapman's sister cried. "I've just finished baking bread, too. I'll fix up something in a jiffy. . . ." She darted into the house.

Chapman put down his young nephew and followed his sister into the house. He looked around the warm kitchen, at the big stone fireplace and the scrubbed board table and chairs. He sat down on one of the chairs and sighed heavily.

"It's great!"

Ed Taylor took out a pouch of tobacco and a corncob pipe. He offered the pouch to Chapman, who shook his head.

"I never really got started."

Anne Taylor was bustling over the cast-iron stove. "Jim, tell us where you've all been. We know you went to Mexico with General Shelby. What was it like down there?"

Chapman's face clouded with unpleasant reminiscence. "Sand, Annie. Sand and sun . . . and a lot of other things."

"Fighting, Jim?" asked Ed Taylor.

"Fighting, Ed. Shelby wanted to throw in with Juarez and the Indian didn't trust him. Well, we couldn't go back, so we went to Maximilian. He was seven hundred miles away and Juarez dogged us every mile. A lot of the boys stayed there in the sand. Of course, you know that Maximilian wouldn't take us either. Not as a body. A lot of us enlisted in his army though when Shelby saw he was licked and disbanded the outfit. I stopped a bullet long before they got Max. . . ."

"Bad?" asked Taylor.

Chapman looked at his sister's back and shook his head. "No . . . not bad. I've been in New York. And Chicago for a while. There's a city that's coming along. It'll beat St. Louis some day, probably New York. If they ever get their streets out of the mud. . . . But what've you been doing, Ed?"

Ed Taylor spread out his hands. "Nothing, Jim. Nothing, but trying to make a few crops grow. I stick to home pretty much. The war's over as far as I'm concerned. No use looking for trouble."

Chapman looked thoughtfully at his brother-in-law. "The Yanks are pretty tough?"

"Not the soldiers. Well, you expect it from them. But the Dutch . . . and the others. . . .I guess they'd like all Southern people to get out of the country and let them grab what's ours. Our horses and cattle. And farms. I mean, it's just as well not to go shouting you're a Confederate."

"I rode the stage from Independence," said Chapman. "Henry Slocum said something and you could have cut the silence after that. They're pretty bitter about . . . us. . . ."

"Clem Tancred's back. Dan's supposed to be in Texas, or somewhere down there. Maybe it's the Indian Nations."

"Clem," mused Chapman. "He left us after Lawrence. Went with Price into Arkansas and Louisiana. How is he, Ed?"

"Bigger than ever. He—he came back in a Confederate uniform. A captain. The Tancreds talked pretty loud about Clem having been a captain under Price and well, there are a lot of Tancreds. . . . But last week someone took a shot at Billy Bligh."

"Billy's back? He went to Kentucky in '65."

"Yes, he got a parole there after Quantrell was killed. He came back last summer. Been in trouble ever since. They had him up for that bank job, but couldn't pin it on him. At least, no one dared identify him."

Chapman's forehead creased. "I read about that in the New York papers. They played it up big. I guess seventy thousand is a lot of money even there. . . . Who was it, Ed?"

Ed Taylor looked at the floor. "Billy hasn't done much farming. And Clem—"

"Clem?" Chapman said, softly. "Clem Tancred."

"I don't know," Ed Taylor said hastily. "There were ten or twelve. They charged down on the bank and began shooting a lot. They weren't masked, but no one admitted having recognized any of them. Not even the Cagels. *They'd* know the boys, wouldn't they?"

"They should. But I don't think they'd want to talk."

"They didn't. At least not in public. Sheriff Gregg didn't do anything until there was some talk about Billy Bligh. He turned him loose, though, the same day. . . ."

Anne Taylor finished setting the table. "Pull up your chair, Jim. You can talk when you've eaten. . . ."

Three

WHEN HE HAD eaten, it was time for Ed Taylor to perform the evening chores. Chapman went with him. He even tried milking one of the two cows and found his fingers stiff from long disuse. Ed finished Chapman's cow for him.

"You're out of practice, Jim. Well, what do you think of it? Can we make a go of the farm?"

"We?"

"It's your farm, Jim. Your dad wanted it for you and Tom. Me, I just sort of moved in. I never owned anything before and—"

"Don't talk nonsense, Ed. This is your place as much as mine. You've run it and you keep on running it. I may not stick around, anyway."

"No? You're not going away again, Jim?"

"I don't know. It's . . . not the same. Maybe I'll get used to it, but right now . . . I feel all hollow, Ed."

"Yeah," said Taylor. "I know. I felt that way when I heard about Order Number 11 and I kept writing to Anne and couldn't get any answer. I knew she was having Tommy and all the news from here was bad. It *was* bad, here."

"*We* were responsible for Order Number 11," Chapman said bitterly. "You'd think we had enough. And now they're still at it. Billy and Clem—"

"Ed Taylor!" called a voice from the house. "Ed Taylor . . . and *Jim Chapman*. Let's see your face, Jim, you old son of a gun. This is Billy!"

Billy Bligh came around the house. He was a year or so older than Jim Chapman. Better filled out, but an inch shorter. He had full mustaches, waxed at the ends and wore a broadcloth suit and a derby hat.

He grinned in huge delight as he rushed forward and caught Jim Chapman in an embrace. "Jim, you old son of a gun. Where've you been? What've you been doing? They couldn't kill you down there, huh?"

"No, they couldn't," laughed Chapman. "But it's a good thing the Mex's didn't see you. You've gotten so fat you'd make an easy mark for them. They couldn't hit anything smaller than the side of a barn."

13

Billy Bligh stepped back and gazed fondly at Chapman. "Jeez, I'm glad you're back. It's like old times. Clem and Dick—Dick Wood, yeah, he's back—and the Welker boys. We'll make some of these goddam Yanks step around yet."

"The same old Billy," said Chapman. "Sooner fight than eat. Didn't you get a bellyful of trouble?"

"You bet! But I've got a big belly. I've been taking them on here, too. Ed tell you about me getting arrested last fall? Ha! They said I held up Old Cagel's bank and stole the money he made selling spoiled beef to the bluecoats." He suddenly caught Jim's eyes and motioned him aside.

Ed Taylor saw the signal and picked up his pail of milk and went to the house with it. Billy Bligh held onto Chapman's arm.

He said in a low tone, "Maybe some fellas you know did pull that job, Jim. You can't tell. Maybe I was even in on it. Huh?"

"Maybe so, Billy."

"They own the country, Jim. They robbed us of everything we had and they kick us around now. A Confederate can't hold any office; he can't even vote or get a white man's job. What's he going to do? Starve? Not me, Jim. I'm going to eat and I like fried chicken sometimes. Jeez, Clem will be glad to see you. He says his brother, Dan, is coming back from Texas in a week or so. Pretty soon we'll have a whole bunch around here, eh?"

Chapman nodded thoughtfully. "Yes, but Billy . . . the war's over. You can't hold up banks, now."

"Why not? They're Yankee banks, ain't they? And anyway, we didn't quit the war. You never signed any parole, did you?"

"Is it necessary? This late?"

Billy Bligh shrugged. "Who gives a damn? There're still more Southern people around here than damyanks. It's only their lousy soldiers that're running things. And their spies that're makin' trouble. That sneakin' neighbor of yours across the road, Hobson, he's a spy. I got my eye on him."

Chapman started slowly toward the house and Billy Bligh walked with him. Anne Taylor came to the doorway and greeted Bligh without warmth.

"Thought you'd be home getting ready for the dance, Billy."

Bligh slapped his broadcloth-covered thigh. "Yep, that's right. I wouldn't miss a dance for anything. And Jim—you're coming, of course?"

Chapman shook his head. "I haven't done much dancing the last few years."

"All the more reason you ought to come tonight. You've got to come, Jim. The boys'll all be there—Clem and Clarence and Dick. And girls—say, you ought to see some of them that have grown up. Maybe the Comstock girl will be there. Prettiest thing in the country. . . ."

Chapman looked past Billy at his sister. "Maybe I will go to the dance. You and Ed going, Anne?"

Anne Taylor shook her head. "I've got out of practice. But . . . well, maybe we will go. I'll get one of the Hobson children to come stay with Tommy." She turned into the house and Chapman heard her talking to Ed about going to the dance.

"I'll see you tonight, then, Jim," Bligh said enthusiastically. "The dance is at the schoolhouse, you know."

After Bligh had gone, Chapman went into the house. Anne began making an early supper and Ed Taylor got a well-thumbed farmer's almanac and began reading. Chapman sat down in an armchair and stretching out his legs regarded the domestic scene with a contentment he had not known in years.

After a while, Ed said without looking up from his almanac, "What do you think of Billy, Jim?"

Chapman shrugged. "He's about the same as always. Maybe he talks a little more. But he always did talk a lot."

Anne turned from the stove with a wooden cooking spoon in her hand. "Billy *was* one of those who robbed the bank. He hasn't done an honest day's work in a year, but he's able to sport fancy clothes. I don't like your taking up with him again, Jim. There's trouble coming for Billy and those who travel with him. You don't want to get mixed in it."

"I'm not looking for trouble, Anne. I just want to take things easy for a while."

"Then keep Billy Bligh away from you. See him tonight, but let him know that you don't put up with his ways. You've had enough trouble. We all have."

Chapman said no more. He was wholly in agreement with his sister's views. He had never particularly liked Billy Bligh, anyway. Clem Tancred, yes, but Clem was a different sort. If there hadn't been a war Clem would probably have become a preacher or a lawyer. He liked to read.

It was still daylight when Ed Taylor hitched up his team to the heavy farm wagon and the three of them got in to go to the dance at Funk's Grove schoolhouse, two miles from the Taylor farm.

As early as they got there, however, there were already a dozen wagons about and the fiddler could be heard inside the schoolhouse tuning up his instrument.

A young giant in a tight-fitting suit came over to the wagon and grasped Chapman's hand as he stepped down.

"Jim!"

"Clem Tancred," Chapman said tightly.

"It's been a long time. I'd heard you'd stopped a bad one down in Mexico, but no one seemed to know what'd become of you. It was hell down there, wasn't it?"

Chapman nodded. "I got enough. From now on I'm going to keep—Dick Wood!"

A slight, bandy-legged man of twenty-two or twenty-three came forward grinning from ear to ear. While Chapman was pounding Wood on the back, the Welker boys arrived. They were twins but Clarence outweighed his brother by twenty pounds and was two inches taller. Yet Clark had always been a few feet in front of Clarence in a fight.

When the greetings were over, Dick Wood said to Chapman, "We got a jug out in the woodshed. C'mon and see if you remember how Missouri corn tastes."

Chapman did not care especially to renew the acquaintance with the Missouri jug but he went with the others and when the jug was handed first to him, in honor of his return, he took a swig of it. It burned and made him cough and the others joked about it.

Billy Bligh arrived then, resplendent in Prince Albert and white silk vest. He even wore a silk hat and had his trousers tucked into a fifty-dollar pair of hand-stitched riding boots.

He took two healthy pulls on the jug and roared. "What a gang of us, now! Like to see those goddam Yanks start anything tonight."

"Mebbe they will," said Clark Welker. "George Pike got here early and he looked like he'd started likkerin' about breakfast time."

"Pike?" asked Chapman. "Who's he?"

Clem Tancred grimaced. "A loud-mouthed corporal from Minnesota. He grabbed Tutt's place and stayed here. Doesn't do any farming, but sells a lot of stock. More than he buys or raises. He's pretty thick with Sheriff Gregg."

Inside the schoolhouse the fiddler and a guitar player struck into a lively dance tune and there was immediate cheering and stamping.

Ed Taylor came to the door of the woodshed. "Hello, fellows," he said. "Anne wants you to dance the first one with her, Jim."

"Of course. Coming, fellows?"

They trooped into the schoolhouse, already well lighted with wall lamps. Chapman found his sister near the door and moved awkwardly out upon the floor with her. Couples swirled around them. Now and then a man yelled at Chapman or clapped him heartily upon the back.

Anne said, "I wouldn't make too many trips out to the woodshed, Jim."

Chapman chuckled. "Going to look after me, Anne?"

"Maybe you need it. You haven't been around women enough, Jim. Now, there's a nice girl over there, Andrew Miller's oldest girl, Sophie. She's already got her eye on you."

Chapman looked where his sister indicated and had a passing glimpse of a girl of sixteen or seventeen. But his eyes came to rest upon another girl . . . Evelyn Comstock. She wore a velvet dress, cut low at the throat, and her blond hair was brushed and coiled smoothly upon the back of her neck. She was looking away from Chapman and he caught her profile, so finely chiseled.

He said to his sister, "Who is the girl in the green velvet?"

Anne twisted sideways in his embrace. "That—that's Evelyn Comstock. Surprised she came here. Guess old Preston wanted to size up what farmer's mortgage he should foreclose tomorrow. He owns the Cagel bank. Took it over when the Cagels had to close. There's her brother over there . . . Captain Cliff Comstock. And don't forget the captain. He was on Kirby Smith's staff."

"She isn't dancing," Chapman said.

Anne Taylor looked up sharply at him. "Take your eyes off her, Jim. She only dances with Martin Halliday, who is almost as rich as her father. Something must have kept him, for he ought to be here."

The musicians stopped and the dancers—and those who weren't dancing, on the fringes—applauded vigorously for an encore. When it began, Chapman saw Pike.

He was standing about eight or ten feet from Evelyn Comstock, flanked by several men whose faces were slightly familiar and had probably been his fellow card players on the train. Pike was glowering at Chapman. When he danced past with his sister, Chapman saw that Pike's face was flushed a deep crimson. As much from drink as anger, no doubt.

Chapman saw his brother-in-law at the edge of the dance

floor and when he came up to him, he surrendered his sister to her husband.

"Out of practice, Anne," he apologized.

Pike was already weaving through the dancers to come to Chapman. When he arrived, he said, "So you're Jim Chapman. Didn't figure I'd see you again."

"You're not much soberer," Chapman retorted curtly.

Pike sneered. "And you're one of these Confederates. I guess they did call themselves Confederates, didn't they? I was at Westport."

"Pike," said Chapman deliberately. "I'm going to be around here for a while. Someday, when you're sober and you feel the same way, come and see me. Until then—" Chapman turned his back and walked toward a corner where Clem Tancred and the others were talking.

Tancred said, "Didn't know you knew George Pike, Jim."

"I met him on the train this afternoon."

"I may kill him someday," Clem Tancred said laconically.

Pike had gone back to his cronies and they went into a huddle. Chapman wondered if they were going to take up the gauntlet he had thrown at them on the train that afternoon.

"I think I'll dance," Clem Tancred announced. "Maybe she'll turn me down." He winked at Chapman and began pushing his way through the dancing couples.

Chapman watched him and was surprised to see Tancred go up to Evelyn Comstock and talk to her. He was even more surprised when he saw her nod and put up her arms for Clem.

Well, perhaps he wasn't so surprised. The Tancred family still owned their land, more than 3,000 acres of it. Before the war Major Tancred had been one of the wealthiest men in the county. He had owned a stage line, hundreds of head of cattle and horses, a livery business in Freedom.

The livestock melted away during the war, and his enterprises were taken over by the Union Army after the major was killed by Kansas soldiers turned murderers. The Tancreds had suffered as much as any Clay County family and Clem as well as his brother had ridden under the black flag. Clem had partially redeemed himself by going with General Price after Lawrence, but Dan had remained with Quantrell, had even gone with him to Kentucky on the last fatal expedition. For that reason he was now living in Texas.

There were only a few minutes left of the encore and at the end of it, a tall, black-haired man in a gray Prince Albert took Evelyn Comstock from Clem Tancred.

Clem came back to Chapman. "She told me about the train

business, Jim. You should have let Pike have it then and saved us all some trouble."

"Who's the tall fellow in the gray Prince Albert?" Chapman countered.

"Her brother, Captain Cliff Comstock; he's in the bank with old Preston. Halliday was called to Kansas City on some business. That's a break for me. I'd never have got to dance with her, otherwise."

Pike and a pair of his friends had broken away from the others in his crowd and were cutting across the dance floor to intercept a square-built man with an iron-gray spade beard.

Pike talked excitedly to the bearded man for a moment and the latter nodded and began searching faces until he saw Clem and then shifted to Chapman.

"I suppose," Chapman said quietly, "that's Gregg, the sheriff with whom my friend Pike is talking?"

"Yeah. And he's coming over here. Maybe he's going to make something. Nah, I guess he wouldn't dare, not here."

Sheriff Gregg came over alone, moving heavily and methodically through the crowd. He greeted Clem Tancred.

"Hello, Clem, havin' a good time?"

"I *was*," Clem retorted.

"I don't know your friend," Gregg said deliberately.

"He's one of the Booths," Tancred said bluntly. "John Wilkes."

Gregg stroked his spade beard. "Name's Chapman, isn't it?" he said to Chapman.

"Yes," Chapman replied. "I saw Pike talking to you. He told you I threw him off the train because he was drunk and disturbing the passengers?"

Gregg shrugged. "Well, he didn't put it quite like that. He said you cut in on a friendly discussion he was having and pulled a Navy on him. You hadn't ought to done that, Chapman."

"That wasn't in Clay County," Chapman said pointedly.

"And if it'd been me, I'd have creased his scalp," Clem Tancred said belligerently.

Like a cat, Gregg stuck out the tip of his tongue and licked the top of his whiskers. "There's too much fightin' talk around here, Clem. Folks don't like it. I've had complaints. In fact, I was coming over to see you tomorrow."

"You're seeing me now!" Tancred challenged.

Gregg shook his head. "Tomorrow'll do." He turned and walked back to where Pike was waiting for him.

Clem swore. "Sanctimonious hypocrite! Let's go and see if

the boys have left anything in the jug. Want to get the bad taste out of my mouth."

There was some left in the jug, but it was not the same one they had sampled before. That one lay empty on the ground inside the woodshed.

Dick Wood and the Welker boys had been passing the second jug around. Clem told them about the brush with the sheriff. Dick Wood chuckled. "Maybe they voted an indictment for you, Clem?"

Clem Tancred slapped Wood's mouth, not too gently. "Don't even joke about that, Dick. I don't like it."

"It's only among our bunch," Dick said sullenly.

"You're getting to talk as much as Billy," Clem Tancred snapped. "Keep your mouth shut."

Outside, Anne Taylor called, "Jim Chapman!"

Chapman stuck his head out of the woodshed. "Yes, Anne?"

"Ed wants to go home; are you coming with us?"

"Hell, the evening's young," Clem said to Chapman.

Chapman shrugged. "My first day home, you know. I could use some sleep. Why not ride over tomorrow, Clem?"

"I will," Clem promised. "If Gregg doesn't come over too soon."

Ed Taylor already had the wagon ready. Chapman helped his sister in, then climbed up himself.

When they were out in the road, Anne said, "I wanted to get you away before the trouble started, Jim. Pike was about to fight the war over again."

Chapman did not tell his sister that it was himself, rather than the Confederates, Pike wanted to fight. He was just as glad to avoid trouble.

He slept that night up in the attic where he and his brother had slept in the old days. He even cracked his head on the old beam beside the old four-poster.

Four

THE ODOR of frying pork and hot coffee awakened Chapman the next morning. He dressed quickly and climbed down the ladder to the kitchen. His sister was cooking breakfast and carrying on a conversation with a slatternly-looking woman of about forty.

"This is Mrs. Hobson, Jim, our neighbor."

Mrs. Hobson examined Chapman with lascivious eyes. "So you're Jim Chapman that we've heard so much about. Why, you're only a boy."

"You have to be a boy before you're a man," Chapman said dryly and went outside where a tin basin and a bucket of water stood on the bench beside the door.

He washed and dried himself on a huck towel hanging from a nail. While he was busy, Mrs. Hobson came out and attempted to carry on a conversation but when Chapman merely grunted replies, she took herself off to her home, out by the main road.

Anne came then and announced that breakfast was ready. She called Ed from his work outside. "Mrs. Hobson brought the gossip," Anne said while the men were eating. "They had a fight at the dance last night. That ruffian Yankee, Pike, slugged Clark Welker and then Clem Tancred blacked both of Pike's eyes. It was all Sheriff Gregg could do to prevent gunplay. . . . It's a good thing we left early. Mrs. Hobson said the fight started because of some things Pike said about you, Jim. I didn't know you knew the man."

"I had a brush with him on the train," Chapman replied. "He was drunk and scaring people. I kicked him off."

Ed Taylor shook his head. "Pike's got a lot of influence around here. He's the leader of the Northern trash that's taken over. Gregg plays up to him and Gregg's brother-in-law, Major Peterson, is the provost marshal."

Chapman ate silently for a while, but when he finished the last of his coffee, he said, "Maybe it was a mistake to come back. I think I'll run over to Kansas City. Man I met on the train offered me a job."

"A job in Kansas City?" exclaimed Anne. "Doing what? You've never worked for anyone."

"Why, this is sort of detective work," Chapman exclaimed.

Ed Taylor gulped and Chapman's sister stared at him. "Detective work. After what—I mean, well, that *is* rather surprising. Who's the man wants to hire you?"

"Alan Vickers."

Ed Taylor whistled softly. "You're not taking the job?"

"Why not? The Vickers outfit is big. The job might work into something pretty good."

"But Vickers is a Yankee!" cried Anne. "He—he furnished all the spies for McClellan. Besides . . ."

Ed Taylor finished for his wife. "The Vickers agency worked on the bank job. They're the ones arrested Billy Bligh, you know. Only they couldn't make it stick."

A cloud came over Chapman's face. "Then one of the cases their new branch office will work on is the Cagel one. Well, I guess that's out then."

Anne Taylor shuddered. "Don't even mention the name Vickers around here these days. Folks won't like it."

Outside, a voice hallooed. Chapman went to the door and greeted Clarence Welker, astride a big chestnut gelding.

"Morning, Clarence."

"Gregg's served a warrant on Clem. I understand he's getting one out for you, Jim."

"Me? What for?"

"Same thing. The Cagel job."

"But I wasn't here when that happened."

Clarence Welker grinned. "*I* know that. So does everyone else. Gregg can't make it stick, but he figures to bother you enough so you'll pull out of here. Pike's behind it, of course."

"Pike!" snapped Chapman. "I should have killed him when I had the chance. . . ."

"Jim!" cried Anne Taylor from the doorway. "Don't talk like that."

Chapman bit his lip. "Is Clem getting bail?"

"Oh, yes! They can't prove anything on him. Nobody's going to get up in a courtroom and testify that Clem Tancred —or anyone else—robbed the Cagel bank. Nobody who figures on living to a ripe old age."

Down the lane came the hoofbeats of a galloping horse. After a moment Clark Welker burst into sight. "Jim!" he cried, "Gregg's comin' here with a posse. Better take to the woods."

"How many are there?"

"Six or seven. Pike and his gang. Gregg's swore them in as deputies."

Chapman nodded. "Let's go talk to them. . . ."

"Jim!" cried Anne Taylor. "Don't you—"

He shook his head and walked off, without looking back. The Welker boys trotted their horses beside him. When they had gone up the lane a little way, Clark Welker said in a low tone, "I haven't got a gun, Jim."

"It's all right, we're not going to fight." His own gun was up in the attic of the house. It was just as well. The war was over and things could no longer be settled with the Navy Colt.

The posse was just turning in from the road, when the trio of former guerrillas met them. The possemen lined up across the lane. Sheriff Gregg said easily: " 'Morning, boys. Out early, aren't you?"

"So're you," retorted Clark Welker.

"I understand you have a warrant for me, Sheriff," Chapman said.

Sheriff Gregg pretended surprise. "Warrant, Chapman? What makes you think that?"

"Have you got one?"

"Of course not. What've you done that I ought to get a warrant for?" He stroked his glossy spade beard. "I did serve a paper on Clem Tancred this morning. But that was for something that happened while you weren't living around here, Chapman."

Pike moved his horse up beside Gregg's. "Go on, Gregg, tell him."

Gregg pretended to have just recalled something that had apparently not been important enough to remember. "Oh, yes . . . yeah, that's right. I was riding by this way, today and Major Peterson, the provost marshal, mentioned that I stop by and tell you to come in and see him."

"What for?"

"Why, I don't know, Chapman. Probably just some red tape, you know. Check up on your parole. Nothing important. Well. . . . I'll be seeing you around, I suppose."

With that the horsemen wheeled and headed back toward Freedom. The Welkers waited until they were out of earshot, then Clark exclaimed, "Be damned! That Gregg is smooth. He's getting his brother-in-law to pull out his chestnuts for him."

"I haven't got a parole," said Chapman. "I never surrendered, you know."

"I guess you'll have to, Jim," said Clarence. "All the Confederates got amnesty."

"Clark," Chapman said. "Mind letting me have your horse?

Think I'll ride in now and get it over with. Go back to the house and tell Anne."

Clark Welker promptly slid from his horse. "Sure, Jim. Take your time. I'll get me some sleeping." He grinned. "Or maybe I'll watch Ed work. That always tired me out."

Clarence Welker and Chapman rode leisurely to Freedom, in order not to catch up with Gregg and his posse. They encountered Clem Tancred on the street, across from the bank. He had already posted bail. He was seething.

"They're carrying things too far, I tell you," he declared. "We're not going to stand for much more. . . . Where you going, Jim?"

"To the provost marshal's. He wants to see me. I haven't surrendered yet, you know."

Clem Tancred frowned. "All right, but Clarence and me'll wait outside. He tries any funny stuff, just you yell!"

"No, Clem," said Chapman. "We're not going to make any trouble. According to the law I've got to surrender and according to the same law he's got to give me my parole."

"Well, we'll wait for you, anyway."

A couple of uniformed soldiers were loafing outside the provost marshal's office. They scowled at the trio of former Confederates, but Welker and Tancred ignored them and seated themselves upon the stairs of a neighboring house.

Chapman went into the provost marshal's office and was kept waiting twenty minutes in an anteroom by a clerk with corporal's chevrons on his blouse. When he finally went into the provost marshal's office, Major Peterson was reading a newspaper with his boots up on a desk.

"Who're you?" he snapped at Chapman.

"James Chapman. I'm applying for a parole."

"Parole? Kind of late for that, aren't you?"

Chapman shrugged and Major Peterson removed his feet from the desk. "Your regiment?"

"Fourteenth Missouri."

"Oh," said Peterson sarcastically. "You're from Shelby's famous brigade, eh? Very romantic. You buried your flag in the Rio Grande, rather than surrender it. Nice sentiment. Well, how long did you serve with Shelby?"

"From October '64 until its disbandment in Mexico City."

Major Peterson took a blank and dipped a pen into an inkwell. He wrote for a moment. "And what was your regiment before October, 1864?"

Chapman looked steadily at the provost marshal. After a

moment, Peterson jerked up his head. "Well? Can't you answer?"

"You know very well what I did before then," Chapman said evenly.

Peterson bared his teeth in a grimace. "Guerrilla, huh? I've got to put it down that way. How long were you with Quantrell?"

"A year and a half."

Major Peterson's pen scratched, then finally he laid it down and put the slip of paper in a seal. He pressed down on it and waved the parole in the air.

"I'm giving this to you, because I have to, Chapman," he said curtly. "But I'm going to do something that I don't have to do. I'm going to warn you about your future actions around here. I don't mind telling you that I served under Lieutenant Colonel Plumb in enforcing Order Number 11 here and in Jackson County and I know all about your crowd. I'm telling you . . . Behave yourself."

"You'll get no trouble from me," Chapman said softly.

"I hope not. One more repetition of what your friends did here a couple of months ago and this country goes under martial law. Real martial law, not what we've got now. It's going to be tough on your crowd then."

Chapman reached forward and took the parole from Peterson's hand, then without a word turned and left the provost marshal's office.

Outside, Clem Tancred and Clarence Welker were still sitting on the stairs next door. Their faces were taut. The Federal soldiers nearby were talking loudly.

"The goddam Rebs," one of them was saying, "I'd give them paroles with the bayonet, that's what I'd do if I had my way. . . ."

"Come on," Chapman said curtly to his friends. They got up quickly.

"Shall I take a poke at them?" Clem Tancred asked.

Chapman took his arm. They crossed the street and got their horses, then rode to the far side of the square. There Tancred stopped and swung from the saddle.

"I'm going in here to have a drink," he said, nodding toward a brick building over which was a sign: *Hoffstetter's Saloon.*

"That's up to you, Clem," said Chapman. "I'm going home. How about you, Clarence?"

Clarence Welker hesitated, then finally sided with Chapman. "Maybe this ain't the time to get liquored up, Clem."

Clem Tancred swore. "If they're looking for trouble, they know where to find me."

Chapman and Clarence Welker rode out of Freedom. Chapman felt oddly depressed. "I don't think we should have left Clem back in town."

"No, maybe not," agreed Welker. "But Clem's got a mighty stubborn streak in him. We'd pressed him and he'd just as likely gone back to pick a fight with those bluecoats. Best to let him work it off by himself."

Five

THEY RODE in silence for a few minutes, then Chapman sighed wearily. "I don't think I like it so well around here. Things have changed too much."

"Sure, they've changed. We lost a war. None of us like that . . . except maybe the Yanks. They won the war. What you figure on doing, Jim?"

"I don't know. I hadn't thought about it much, except to come home. I can see now that it isn't going to work out. I may try it farther West. They're sending cattle up from Texas and it may develop into something big. I don't know, it might be a good thing to see what's in it. . . ."

"Oh-oh," said Clarence. "Look, what's coming."

Ahead, a hundred yards, a group of horsemen had come around a turn in the road. They were wearing blue uniforms. Snatches of boisterous song came to Chapman and Welker.

"Best keep our mouths shut," Welker cautioned.

The soldiers had seen them. The song stopped and the men seemed to be arguing among themselves. Then a voice yelled, "Rebels!"

"Easy!" Welker snapped in a low tone.

"You—eee!" yipped one of the soldiers.

Then a gun roared.

Clarence Welker jerked and let out a groan. Shocked, Chapman lunged his horse over to his friend. Clarence was fumbling under his coat, for his revolver.

He was cursing. "Goddam them, the dirty sons of—!"

Something tugged at Chapman's coat and he was aware that two or three guns were now barking. "To the woods, Clarence!" he cried.

He reached out to catch Welker, but Clarence's body missed his grasp and tumbled to the road. The Navy Colt that had been cleared from Clarence's belt thudded to the dust a couple of feet away. Stooping, Chapman's eyes were riveted on the gun.

In that instant that he looked at the gun, he tried to make a decision. His hand swooped down for the gun but in the moment of closing upon it, he swept his hand sidewards and began straightening in his saddle.

He never quite made it. His borrowed horse suddenly screamed and reared up on its hind legs. Chapman was thrown from its back and landed in the road on his side, narrowly missing the plunging animal's hoofs.

Hoofs pounded the hard earth, the soldiers yelled wildly and a bullet kicked up dirt two feet from Chapman. He came up to his hands and knees, gasped when he saw that the soldiers were almost upon him and scuttled for the underbrush at the edge of the road.

"Get him!" a raucous voice roared.

A bullet clipped a twig from a bush in front of his face. Chapman lunged headlong for shelter. Enraged that he seemed to be escaping, the soldiers fired a volley at him. Then a tree seemed to fall and strike Chapman to the earth. He fell into a hazel bush and was vaguely aware that his face was gashed by a broken branch.

But he felt no pain. A numbness had taken possession of him and a great weight pressed him down to the earth.

From far off, he heard someone cry out, "I got him, the dirty Rebel bastard!"

The earth under his hands was moving backwards. It must have been the earth that moved, for Chapman knew that he was not propelling himself. He heard thrashing among the bushes behind him and wanted desperately to scramble away.

Guns were still banging, but the reports were farther away. A wall of green laurel rushed down upon him and enveloped him in its massive greenery. It deadened all sound around him and not until then did he become aware that it wasn't the earth at all that was moving. It was himself, crawling on hands and knees like a wounded wolf.

The weight on his back was disappearing, to be replaced by pain that racked his entire body. He had been hit by a bullet. So had Clarence Welker. But Clarence was back there on the road, with a revolver near his hand.

Chapman was unarmed. And the drunken soldiers were beating the woods for him, firing into bushes and clumps of laurel. They had to get him, now. They couldn't leave a wounded man to testify against them.

A huge beast was floundering near by. Chapman slipped to the ground and lay at full length. Black, polished boots appeared before his eyes, ten feet away. Above the boots was a pair of blue trousers, with yellow stripes down the seams.

Chapman strained his eyes upwards, without moving his head and saw the twisted, bestial face of Pike.

Pike in a cavalryman's uniform. Pike, who had been discharged from the army two years ago. He was wearing a uniform now, carried a Navy Colt in his fist and he was searching for the wounded Chapman, to dispatch him.

He couldn't see Chapman because all but his face was concealed in the laurel, but he knew that Chapman must be somewhere about.

"Chapman!" he called, "show your face, so I can put a bullet in it. You dirty—guerrilla. You were so cocky yesterday. Come out and fight like a man, now."

And Chapman lay in the laurel, bleeding.

From the rear, a voice yelled to Pike. "Come on, George, we've got to get out of here. People'll be coming along. . . ."

Pike called back, in a frenzy. "I want Jim Chapman, the—! He's around here somewhere."

"Let him go," the voice replied. "You saw him fall. He won't get far. This one's a goner. . . ."

Pike's legs disappeared but Chapman heard him thrashing around for a few minutes more. Then, gradually, silence descended upon the forest.

Chapman placed his hands flat on the ground and attempted to raise his body to a crawling position. Red pain exploded in his body, forcing a groan from his lips. He fell back to his face and lay for long moments, gathering sufficient strength for another attempt. He made it the second time and after a moment during which he fought nausea, pulled himself forward, out of the laurel to a poplar tree. He grasped this and with its help began pulling himself to his feet.

When he succeeded he clung to the tree for a while, before forsaking it. He surprised himself, then, by walking to a tree twenty feet away. He steadied himself on that one for a moment, then essayed the venture again, walking thirty feet or more.

He continued the process and after a little while was able to walk without stopping at all. After five minutes or so, he came to a small, cool stream. He waded it and saw ahead a clearing.

A woman in a gingham dress and a huge sunbonnet was working among some rose-bushes. Shortly behind her was a big, red-brick house, with white pillars. Chapman did not recognize the house. It must have been built since the war and by its size, it probably belonged to a Yankee carpetbagger. The woman. . . .

She straightened and he saw that it was Evelyn Comstock. She was holding a big pair of shears and staring at him. He took a step forward, then missed the ground with his foot and fell forward on his face. That was all he knew for some time.

Six

CHAPMAN DREAMED that he had been hiding in a cave and that it had fallen in on him and he was smothering under the earth. He clawed at it, but it filled his eyes and mouth and his frantic digging only brought more of the stuff down on him.

And then his eyes opened and he saw through a thin layer of hay over his eyes, the blue sky and the bright, radiant sun. He heard creaking of wheels and as one of them hit a rut he was jolted so that pain lanced through his body.

He was lying in a moving wagon, covered loosely with hay. He recalled suddenly the last thing that had happened to him before unconsciousness had swooped over him and he clawed the hay from his face.

Evelyn Comstock turned on the seat directly over him and said: "Better keep down. It's only another mile."

He stared upward at her face. It was calm, but her eyes were wide and her lips seemed to be twitching lightly. He said, "You . . . put me in here?"

"One of our boys helped me. I thought it safer, however, to drive you myself. There's trouble."

"I know. They killed Clarence Welker. . . ."

She nodded. "Clem Tancred killed a soldier in town."

Chapman groaned. "They've arrested him?"

"No. He got away. He's—he's at Fothergill's . . . where I'm taking you. You—well, you may as well know the worst. The soldiers claim *you* killed Welker. They said you left Freedom with him, that you shot him and—"

Chapman shook his head in bewilderment. "Then why are *you* going to all this. . . ."

She looked ahead on the road. "You interceded for me yesterday, without even knowing me. This is the least I can do in return."

"But you'll get in trouble."

"No one will know. Our boy will keep silent. And—your sister says Fothergill is to be trusted."

"You talked to her?"

"I sent word by Rupe. Your sister said to take you to Fothergill's, because the sheriff had some men watching near

31

your home. . . ." She was silent for a moment, then, "It's been a rather sorry homecoming for you, hasn't it?"

Chapman laughed bitterly. "I should have stayed away. They haven't forgotten the war."

"No," she said, "they haven't. You . . . is it true?"

"That I rode with Bloody Bill Anderson? I did. I was sixteen years old and—"

Evelyn Comstock exclaimed. "Oh, you don't have to explain to me. My brother was in the Confederate Army and we lived in Johnson County then. Mother took me to Nebraska when they issued Order Number 11. She . . . died just after getting there. It was three months before father found me. . . . You'd better cover yourself now. I'm turning in at Fothergill's."

Chapman pulled hay over his face as the wagon bounced over the stub of a dead log. After a moment, the wagon stopped and Evelyn Comstock called, "Mr. Fothergill!"

Jed Fothergill came to the wagon and helped Chapman to the ground. Fothergill was an emaciated man six and a half feet tall, with a death's-head face. He said, "This's been mighty fine of you, Miss Comstock. The boys won't forget it. . . ."

"It was the least I could do," she replied in a low tone. She started to turn the team to go back and her eyes met Chapman's—and dropped.

He said, "Thanks. I hope . . . I'll see you again!"

He was looking after her, when Fothergill beside him, said, "The bastards."

Chapman roused. "Clem's here?"

"Yeah. An hour ago. Here he comes. . . ."

Clem Tancred came around the side of the log cabin, a Navy Colt in his hand. He said, "You were right about not staying in town, Jim. But—"

"But I got it just the same," Chapman finished.

"You didn't pack a gun, Jim."

"Clarence had one. He didn't get to use it. They opened up on us without giving us a chance. It was Pike and his gang, wearing uniforms."

Clem Tancred's big face became hard. "Pike in a uniform, eh? So it was all set for us. They knew you'd be coming along that road and figured I'd be with you. I guess this evens things for the Cagel job. . . ."

"Wait a minute," said Fothergill. "I don't want to hear anything about that. Less I know the better."

"Sure, Jed. You go along home. I'll look after Jim." Clem

Tancred came forward and put his muscular arm about Chapman. "We'll go back here and take a look at that wound."

A hundred yards behind Fothergill's house, Clem Tancred had dumped a pile of army blankets and a Sharp's rifle. Chapman spread himself on one of the blankets and Tancred removed his blood-soaked shirt and examined the wound.

"It's not so bad, Jim," he said. "The bullet's in, but it's not touching any bone and it's just as well to leave it. I'll get some clean rags from Jed and wash it up."

A half hour later, when Clem had bandaged the wound, Clark Welker and Billy Bligh came back to the hiding place. Welker was grim and taciturn, but Billy Bligh was loud in his denunciations.

"They're asking for it and they're going to get it. They think we're licked and we're going to take anything laying down. Goddammit, it wasn't us that surrendered. There's just as many Confederates around here as there ever were and they're goddam fed up with being pushed around. The Nigger-lovng bastards, we'll fix them. . . ."

"Billy," Chapman said from his bed on the blankets. "You talk too much with your mouth."

Clem Tancred grunted. "That goes for me, too."

"Hell, I'm only sayin' what you fellows are thinking. Look what they did to Clarence, and you, Jim. They'll do the same to the rest of us. They're out now lookin' for Clem on a murder warrant. They'll shoot him down like a dog. . . ."

"They have to catch me first."

Clark Welker said suddenly, "I'm not going to wait for them to get me."

Chapman rolled his head to look at the surviving twin. "Think it over first, Clark," he said.

"I have. I'm going to get Pike and Gregg. Two for one. That'll make it even."

"I'll get me four," Bligh announced.

Chapman sighed wearily. "How much money have you got left from the Cagel bank, Billy?"

Bligh colored. "Not much. Why?"

"Because you must have had five or six thousand as your share. When you've gone through it all, you'll pull another job. . . ."

"Well, why not? They won't let any of us work."

"How about you, Clem?" Chapman asked.

"I put my share into the farm. Lot of good it'll do me now. Dan's supposed to get here from Texas this week. He won't dare show his face. We'll just have to let the farm go."

"Me, I think I'll go to Texas," said Clark Welker. "After I get Pike and Gregg."

"Texas, yeah!" cried Billy Bligh. "We'll all go there. They say there's money to be made down there in cattle. Why don't we all throw in together and buy us a big ranch?"

"I'm willing," said Clem Tancred. "Dan says it's good country down there. You can pick up cattle at three dollars a head and sell it for twenty up in Kansas. He's coming up to talk me into going back with him. He says all he needs to get a good start is a few thousand dollars. . . ."

Chapman laughed bitterly. "You're all talking around the ring. Why don't you jump into the middle and say what you're going to do: hold up another bank."

Even Billy Bligh was silent for a moment then. Chapman looked around the circle of faces. "That's what you're going to do, isn't it?"

Clem Tancred said, "You're with us?"

"Don't I *have* to be with you? I came home with fourteen dollars. I stopped a bullet. How the hell am I going to get to Texas, or hell, without any money?"

Billy Bligh yelped. "That's the stuff, Jim. We'll show them, the—"

"The bastards!" said Chapman. "We're going to hit back at the Yankees by holding up a bank." His mouth twisted contemptuously. "Yah!"

Ed Taylor came after dark. He brought Chapman his Navy Colt. "Sorry, Jim. Anne's pretty worried, but she says for you to lay low. Why don't you take a trip to St. Louis, for a while, until this blows over?"

"Do you think it'll blow over, Ed?"

"I don't know. I only hope it doesn't get any worse."

"Have they been around?"

Ed Taylor shrugged. "They didn't come to the house, but I heard them in the woods. Two or three at least."

"They didn't follow you?"

"I don't think so."

After Taylor had gone, Fothergill came into the woods. "Couple fellows rode by a little while ago. Do you think it's all right?"

"We'd better move."

"Can you make it, Jim?" Clem asked.

"Sure. A couple of miles, anyway. It feels all right since you bandaged it. We oughtn't to stay too long in one place, anyway."

Seven

BILLY BLIGH and Clark Welker suggested the Comstock Bank in Freedom. "They'd never figure on the same place being held up again," Bligh argued.

Clem Tancred immediatey told what Evelyn Comstock had done for Chapman and that ruled out the Comstock Bank.

Chapman said, "It ought to be farther away, even though we are heading for Texas. We've all got relatives around here and no telling what they'll do to them, if they know it was our bunch."

"The Richfield Bank's got more money than any around," said Tancred. "And a Yankee owns it. An old Kansas man. Captain Shafter he calls himself, but I know damn well he was with Jennison at Independence."

The die cast, there remained only the ironing out of the details. Richfield was on the Missouri River. The logical route of escape was south. It was Confederate country. The Yankees were tolerated down there only because they controlled the law. The farther north, the more Unionists. A bank job would naturally be attributed to former Confederates and pursuit would be in a southern direction.

Chapman suggested they had north to the Iowa line, cross it and then work westward to Nebraska and south through Kansas.

"We'll cut the telegraph wire on the south road and they'll be sure we did it to keep them from sending word in that direction. We won't touch the wire on the north road and take our chances."

He flexed his left shoulder. It was still a little stiff, but the ten days' rest since the Freedom affair had healed it so it no longer pained him.

They made camp in the canebrakes in the bottoms a few miles west of Richfield. They did not build a fire and when morning came, Chapman's shoulder was so stiff he could scarcely raise his left arm. But he did not tell the others about it.

They were pretty sober, anyway.

At the edge of town, they separated, Clem and his brother,

Dan, a year and a half younger, riding ahead and Chapman following after a few minutes' interval, with Welker and Bligh.

The Tancreds tied their horses at the hitch rail in front of the Richfield post office and Chapman led the others past a hundred feet to the Richfield Hotel. They dismounted and fastened the reins about the rail, using slipknots, so they could untie them quickly.

Chapman looked at his nickel-plated watch. "Twelve minutes," he said. "We give them five minutes to open up."

Billy Bligh was tugging nervously at his newly grown mustache. "Damn the waiting," he muttered.

"Go inside and buy yourself some cigars," Chapman suggested.

Bligh accepted the suggestion and Chapman and Welker remained outside on the wooden sidewalk, conversing quietly and looking in every direction but toward the bank, two doors up the street.

After a couple of minutes, Bligh came out of the hotel, with a cold cigar stuck in his mouth. His face was ashen.

"Captain Comstock and his sister are in the hotel," he whispered hoarsely to Chapman. "They were eating breakfast in the dining room and saw me."

"Did you talk to them?"

"No, I made off I didn't see them. Is it off? . . ."

Chapman looked at his watch. It was three minutes after eight. Up the street, the Tancreds were already moving toward the bank.

"Too late," he said. "Come on."

According to prearrangement, Clark Welker walked to the horses and mounted his own. Bligh and Chapman moved leisurely toward the bank. Before they reached it, Clem entered and Dan Tancred, pretending to recognize Chapman as an old friend, hailed him.

"Mike Morrison!" he exclaimed holding out his hand.

Bligh merely nodded to Dan and walked past him to the horses of the Tancreds. Chapman pumped Dan Tancred's hand, then apparently pulled him toward the back.

They passed inside together and saw Clem Tancred at the teller's window. Clem was saying:

"I'd be obliged, sir, if you could cash this bill for me."

The teller picked up the fifty-dollar note that Clem had laid on the counter and examined it. "Certainly, sir. How would you like it?"

The cashier was to the front of the teller, seated in his

railed enclosure, talking to a customer of the bank, an elderly farmer in a linen coat.

Clem reached under his coat and plucked out a Navy Colt.
He thrust it at the startled teller. "I'll have it in big bills.
Along with all the other bills you've got in the place."

Jim Chapman whipped out his gun and covered the cashier
and his customer. "Sorry, gentlemen, but this is a holdup. If
you'll raise your hands, no one will be hurt."

"Up with them!" thundered Bligh, bringing out not one,
but two revolvers.

The bank cashier was staring at them with bulging eyes.
His jaw fell open wide enough to swallow a fist. The farmer,
whose back was turned, whirled around and bleated, "Don't
shoot me! I've got a family and I voted for George Mc-
Clellan. . . ."

"No one's going to be hurt," Chapman reassured them.
"You, Mr. Cashier, please to open your vault. . . ." He
vaulted the low railing and whipped out a folded wheat sack
from under his vest.

He moved toward the rear of the bank, with the frightened
cashier. The door of the vault was closed, but not locked.
The cashier pulled open the heavy door.

Chapman gestured with his Navy Colt and the man stepped
inside and began taking down stacks of currency from a shelf.
Chapman tossed him the wheat sack and the cashier stuffed
in the money. Finished with the bills he attacked a tray of
silver, but Chapman called him off.

"Too heavy, this will do."

Out in the bank, the teller had prepared all the counter
money, under Clem Tancred's persuasion. Chapman scooped
it into the sack, then tossed the thing over the wire screen
to Tancred.

"All right, Joe," he said.

"Jim!" cried Dan Tancred, from near the door. "Bill's in
trouble."

Chapman's eyes darted to the window. Directly outside,
Billy Bligh was wrestling with a heavy-set man. Even as he
looked the stranger shoved Bligh away from him and groped
for his hip.

Bligh sprang forward with clubbed revolver, changed his
mind and fired it instead. The big man reeled back.

Chapman swore under his breath. "Let's go!" he cried.

The Tancreds rushed for the door. Chapman followed, but
turned to call back to those in the bank. "Better not come outside for a minute," he cautioned.

He plunged through the door just as a shotgun roared on the other side of the street. Bligh turned and fired two shots in return, missing the man with the shotgun, but shattering a store window behind him.

The Tancreds ran for their horses and Chapman caught Bligh's arm. "Come on, you fool!" he snarled.

Clark Welker, astride his horse, began firing coolly up the street, not aiming at anyone, but merely to discourage rash citizenry.

As Chapman and Bligh came abreast of the hotel, the door was kicked outwards and the hotel clerk, with an apron about his waist, popped out with a huge Sharp's rifle in his hands. Billy Bligh fired at him, missed and charged the hotel man, just as the latter brought the rifle to his shoulder.

Chapman groaned, stopped, and threw down with his Colt. The gun bucked his palm and the hotel man cried out more in terror than pain. The rifle dropped from his hands, hit the step and blasted out a window across the street. The hotel clerk wrapped his hands around his knee and sat down on the steps.

Behind him, Captain Cliff Comstock stepped out of the hotel, a revolver in his hand. He aimed it at Chapman, then seemed to recognize him and hesitated. While he paused Evelyn Comstock came running out and pushed up her brother's gun hand.

Across a distance of a dozen feet, Chapman's eyes met Evelyn's. He saw fright—and loathing—in her glance. And then he turned away.

Guns were firing generally up the street now, as merchants fired from their doorways. But their courage was superior to their marksmanship. The Tancreds thundered up on their horses as Chapman swung into the saddle.

Clem Tancred ripped the morning air with the old guerrilla yell. It was instantly taken up by Clark Welker and Billy Bligh.

"Yip-yip-yow-eeee!" It was a bloodcurdling scream of hate and defiance. The citizens of Richfield remembered it well from the old days and, in the lull of silence that followed the yell, the former guerrillas, turned bank robbers, thundered down the street.

Eight

ESCAPE WAS ridiculously easy. The guerrillas had roamed this country all during the war. They were masters of the art of hiding a trail and they took advantage of every bit of cover and shelter. They could hide with their horses in a scrap of cover while a troop of Federals passed within ten yards of them, without sighting them.

They laid up by day and traveled by night. They forded streams and went two and three days with no more food than a bird would eat.

They preferred traveling in blinding rains when few others would venture out. They dug potatoes from a field and ate them raw and stripped green ears of corn from their stalks.

On the second day after the Richfield Bank holdup, Chapman rode boldly into a village just above the Iowa line and bought a newspaper.

The affair was still important news.

"Daring Robbers Steal $40,000 in Daylight Holdup."

That was gross exaggeration. The currency in the wheat sack had totaled only a little more than $15,000. Three thousand apiece.

In their bivouac that night, Chapman suggested the old guerrilla strategy—disbandment.

"They know it was five of us and they'll be looking for that number. We've kept out of sight so far, but as the days go on, we'll get careless. Somebody, somewhere, will look on us with suspicion and get to talking. We'll do better to break up."

"But what about Texas?" asked Clem Tancred.

"Not me!" hooted Billy Bligh. "I'm headin' for St. Louis to have a good time. There's more where this come from and I'm not figurin' on saving for my old age—not yet."

"And you, Clark?" Chapman asked of Welker.

Welker shrugged. "I got an uncle in Kentucky, I figure to pay him a visit."

Clem Tancred groaned. "I'm still going to Texas with Dan and give that cattle stuff a whirl. You coming along, Jim?"

Chapman thought of the fifteen-hundred-mile overland trip. It would mean six weeks of strenuous riding. The last couple of nights of traveling had made his shoulder so sore he could scarcely move his left arm.

He shook his head. "I think I'd like to take things easy for a while."

"Where? You can't go back to Freedom. They don't mention our names in that paper, but they'll get around to it, after a while. It wouldn't be safe. . . ."

"I'm not going back to Freedom. I think I'll—" he glanced at Billy Bligh—"I think I'll travel up to Minnesota for a while. It's cool up there in summer."

They separated that night, with more or less vague instructions for communicating with one another at a later date.

Chapman sold his horse the following day to a blacksmith in a small village, for about one third of what the animal was actually worth. He traveled by stagecoach to Burlington and there bought a ticket on the train to Chicago.

Chicago was a yawning metropolis. Thirty years an incorporated city, it was already rivaling St. Louis in population. In bustle it had surpassed it even before the war.

There were blocks and blocks of stores, separated by chasms of mud or dust, depending on the weather, that were designated as streets. In places, the wooden sidewalks, built in a more or less uniform level, were four feet above the streets. It was a city of lumber and tar paper. There were fewer brick buildings than in any metropolis of half its size. In four years more a fire would sweep through the flimsy city and in its ashes would rise a permanent city of brick and stone, larger and more substantial.

Chapman rented a room at the Palmer House. His rough clothing, wrinkled and splattered with dried mud, was not too conspicuous. There were men here from the plains. You saw them now and then walking down the street, wearing buckskin. Cowboys from Texas clumped along the boardwalks.

Chapman went the first day of his stay in Chicago and bought an entire new outfit, Prince Albert coat with a small velvet collar, brocaded black-silk vest, gray-striped trousers and fine calfskin boots. He compromised, however, on a flat-crowned felt hat, rather than wear a derby or silk hat. Then he bought two heavy white silk shirts.

He bought a vest three sizes too large for him and strapped his broad leather belt, in which he carried his Navy Colt, under it.

Having bought his finery, he spent the next week in his

hotel room, sleeping and resting. He went out only for brief walks, during which time he bought newspapers and a book or two which he read from cover to cover in his hotel room.

In the second week, the inactivity began to pall on him and he began to go about the city. At a livery stable, he rented a hack and a fast trotter and drove north across the river to the Old Kinzie house. The prairie began just beyond but for another mile the countryside was dotted with realtors' signs, which advertised—somewhat hopefully, it seemed to Chapman—that Chicago was growing and would soon be spreading out here to Lake View.

Another day he drove out to the site of Fort Dearborn and poked among the old ruins. The third day he drove west to Goose Island and spent an interesting hour talking to a man who made his living trapping muskrats.

Before the end of the second week, he took to spending hours in the bar of the Palmer House, sipping at glasses of cool beer. He liked to lean against the bar and listen to the commercial drummers tell tall stories. He bought an occasional drink for barroom acquaintances and accepted some from others.

One of these, a cadaverous-looking man with a sallow skin and soft, white hands came into the bar every afternoon and spent two or three hours there, although he seldom drank more than two glasses of whisky.

During their third conversation, the stranger introduced himself to Chapman. "My name is Philip Castlemon. I'm in the wheat business."

Chapman had already considered the matter of names and he gave one he had selected for such a contingency—the one with which he had signed the hotel register. "I'm James Blake. I'm newly arrived from California."

"California? Ah, you weren't in the war?"

"I'm sorry to say I wasn't."

"You didn't miss anything." Castlemon tapped his chest. "Eighteen months in Libby. It didn't help my lungs any."

"I've heard of Libby Prison," said Chapman. "I was laid up on my back a spell. A bullet in a mining camp."

Castlemon's eyes lit up. "Gold, sir? A fascinating metal. I contemplated a bit of prospecting myself at one time. Too rigorous. However, you must come down to the Board of Trade with me someday. I'll wager you'll find it almost as interesting as a mining camp."

"I don't understand. Didn't you say wheat, sir?"

Castlemon chuckled. "Yes. But I don't raise it. I merely

speculate in it. The market's rather dull this week, so I haven't been spending much time on the Street. Would you like to go down with me? We can still catch an hour or so of it."

"Why, I think it might be very interesting. If you're sure I'm not putting you out . . ."

"Not at all. I really should go down there and give some instructions to my pit man."

Together they left the hotel and Castlemon signaled to a hansom cab. After a short ride through the dusty streets they dismounted before an imposing edifice on LaSalle Street, Castlemon nodded to a man at the door and they went in.

The scene that greeted Chapman's eyes caused him to blink. It was one of wildest confusion. In two or three clumps on the big floor throngs of men were yelling at the top of their voices, all the while they gesticulated and milled about.

"The pits," Castlemon explained. "The one with the biggest crowd is the wheat. Then there's the oat pit yonder, the corn over there and the smallest one, for provisions. Wheat gets the biggest play here."

"But what are they yelling about? Some of them look pretty excited."

"They are. Did you hear that old fellow with the white goatee? He said, 'Sell one hundred bids May wheat at fifty-seven and three-quarters.' That means he wants to sell a hundred bids at fifty-seven and three-quarters cents a bushel. A bid consists of five thousand bushels."

"What?" exclaimed Chapman. "He wants to sell a half million bushels of wheat? Where did he he get all that wheat?"

"Oh, he doesn't own it. No one actually owns the wheat they buy and sell here. They merely deal in futures. Let's say you want to buy a hundred bids of wheat on a one-point margin. You pay one hundred dollars for that. If the price goes up a point you earn a hundred dollars. If it goes down a point you lose the hundred."

Chapman looked blank for a moment. Then he exclaimed, "Why, that's plain gambling!"

"Of course! No one said it wasn't. The big operators buy on a wider margin. Ten, even fifteen points. Three or four of them get together and form a pool. They buy as much wheat as they can. Then they run the price up. Pretty soon they own all the wheat in sight. In a case like that, not a bushel leaves a warehouse or elevator except at whatever price they set. When the wheat's cornered, there's a scramble.

Everyone wants to buy. Then suddenly, the big fellows dump it on the market. They bet wheat will go low . . . and clean up that way, too."

"What happens when they corner the wheat and run the price up?"

"Then you pay two cents more for a loaf of bread."

Chapman looked thoughtfully at Castlemon. Then he shook his head. "It sounds like a dirty business."

"You never said a truer word, Mr. Blake. Every time I make a thousand dollars here I know I'm stealing it from someone. But . . . that's life. The Confederates stole several years of my life. It all evens up in the end."

"Perhaps it does," Chapman said soberly.

"I'll show you how this works. Yesterday I bought some wheat at fifty-eight. It's selling right now at fifty-seven and three quarters. Watch what happens." He led Chapman to a small booth where a man with an eyeshade and rolled-up sleeves was scribbling on a pad of paper.

"Hello, John," he greeted the man. "Sell a thousand bids of May wheat for me."

"Any price, Mr. Castlemon?"

"Fifty-seven—No, change that. Sell a thousand bids at fifty-six and three quarters."

"Right!" The clerk tore off a slip of paper and waved it at a messenger boy who was hovering near by. The boy rushed madly to the pit, searched around a moment in the milling throng, then thrust the paper into a man's hand. The recipient of the paper glanced at it and crumpled it into a pocket. Then he held up his fist, thumb pointing down.

He turned and attacked the throng and for a moment or two it seemed to Chapman that the shouting increased in tempo. Then the man emerged from the crowd and made a signal.

Castlemon smiled. "Well, I just made twelve hundred and fifty dollars, Mr. Blake."

"But you sold at a lower price than you bought!"

"Of course. I always do. I'm a bear. A bull plays the rising market. I seldom do. So that makes me a bear. Shall we return now to the hotel and celebrate my good—" his mouth twisted sardonically—"my good fortune!"

And Jim Chapman had thrust his gun into a man's face and become an outlaw, for three thousand dollars. He thought about that as he rode back to the Palmer House with Philip Castlemon.

They had dinner together that evening in the ornate hotel

dining room. Chapman had never seen so many well-dressed women in his life, but despite their finery, there was no woman in the room as beautiful as—as Evelyn Comstock. He frowned as he made the mental comparison.

After dinner, Castlemon met a couple of his friends in the hotel lobby. He introduced Chapman as from California and after a few minutes' conversation one of the men asked Chapman if he ever played poker. Chapman admitted that he did.

"Why don't you and Phil come along, then?" the man asked. "We're on our way to enjoy a little game, now. Not a steep one though, as you Californians would judge poker."

Castlemon looked at Chapman. "What do you say, Mr. Blake?"

"Well, I haven't played much lately, but I don't mind sitting in. Provided you gentlemen remember that *I'm* not in the wheat business."

Castlemon chuckled. "If that's all that's worrying you, I'll cut you in on a small deal tomorrow. I've been watching the weather reports. It's been raining in Iowa."

"What does that mean?"

Castlemon moved his thumb up and down. "They've had virtually a drought out there and it's held the price of wheat up unseasonably. I think it'll drop two points tomorrow when it becomes known that it's raining in Iowa."

By this time the quartet had adjourned to the sidewalk and engaged a hansom cab. They drove north across the river and after a block or two the cab stopped before a handsome white-pillared house on State Street.

"Watch Al's game, Mr. Blake," Castlemon cautioned jokingly. "He draws to inside straights."

Nine

A BUTLER OPENED the door for them and a heavy-set man in his early forties came forward and greeted them enthusiastically.

A shock stiffened Jim Chapman. Their host was Alan Vickers, the detective. For a moment, he fought down an impulse to turn and dash out of the house. But then it was too late. Castlemon was introducing him and Vickers held out a muscular hand.

"Mr. Blake of California? Glad to make your acquaintance . . ." He blinked at Chapman. "Haven't I met you somewhere?"

"That pleasure has been denied me," Chapman said stiffly. "I've only just come to Chicago this week."

"I know, but somewhere else. I get around a lot. Mmm . . . I almost never forget a face, yet—" He smiled suddenly and turned briskly to lead them into a card room, where a table and chairs had already been arranged.

"A drink, gentlemen? Wilton . . . the port!"

Castlemon and one of the others immediately peeled off their coats. "Clearing the deck for action," Harvey Sutton declared.

"Go ahead, I always play better in my shirt sleeves, myself," Alan Vickers said.

Chapman looked frostily at Alan Vickers, then deliberately peeled off his Prince Albert and unbuttoned his extra-size vest. He tapped the broad leather belt that was exposed under the vest.

"I'm sorry. A wretched California habit."

Castlemon regarded him in shocked surprise. "You mean you've been carrying around that young cannon all day?"

"At home a man's undressed without one." Chapman unbuckled the belt and wrapped it around the holster in which reposed the big Navy Colt.

Harvey Sutton winced as he sized up the gun. "Aren't you afraid that thing'll go off on you, some time?"

Chapman shook his head and smiled. He hung the outfit on the coat rack with his Prince Albert. Then he took his place at the poker table.

Vickers brought out several packs of cards and seated himself. "I'm going to give you a run for your money tonight, boys. I just opened a new branch in Missouri and I've a hunch it's going to do mighty well for the agency."

Pomeroy grimaced. "Missouri. That's among the rebels, isn't it?"

Vickers laughed. "The war's over, Elton. There are more people in Missouri than there are in Illinois. They had it pretty tough there and Missourians in general are content to take things easy these days."

"Easy?" exclaimed Castlemon. "What about all those bank robberies they've been having down there?"

"There've only been two. And I don't think there'll be any more. They caught one of the bandits and they'll soon have the others."

"You caught the bandit, Al?" Pomery asked.

"A man from my St. Louis office. He picked him up in St. Louis. It seems this bandit was trying to drink St. Louis dry and became a little careless in his talk. He turned out to be a former Confederate—a man named Bligh."

Bligh, the poor, loud-mouthed fool.

Chapman said, "Well, shall we begin, gentlemen?" And thought: He's playing with me. He recognized me and knows that I was one of the men at Richfield.

Vickers said, "I suppose it'll be the usual draw? But since you're new in our game, Mr. Blake, suppose you suggest the limit?"

Chapman shrugged. "What do you usually play?"

Castlemon answered. "We'll forget that this evening. Since you're my guest, we'll play whatever you wish. Say, five dollars?"

Chapman inhaled softly. "Well, gentlemen, five dollars is all right with me. Back home—in California—they generally play the sky, but as for myself—"

"The sky!" exclaimed Pomeroy. "Swell. I don't like a limit game myself. Hurts a man's initiative, I always say."

"Table stakes, then," suggested Vickers. "Your usual stack, Elton?"

"For the beginning, yes. Two thousand."

A tiny frown creased Chapman's forehead. This *was* fast company. He laughed and said, "I didn't know I was going to play tonight, so I didn't stop at the bank. But I'll begin with twenty-five hundred."

He knew that he had less than twenty-six hundred altogether. He brought the money out and shoved it carelessly across the table. Vickers counted it and pushed back seventy-eight dollars. "Hold on to the change, Mr. Blake."

Castlemon contented himself with two thousand dollars' worth of chips, but Harvey Sutton plunged to the extent of three thousand. He also won the deal and promptly anted up ten dollars. The others followed suit.

"Jacks or better," Sutton announced.

Vickers looked at his cards and promptly passed. Pomeroy squeezed his cards, scowled and opened the pot for twenty-five dollars. Castlemon stayed. Chapman tossed in a red chip and followed it with a blue. "I'll have to raise that, gentlemen!"

All eyes came to him. He smiled.

Sutton looked over his cards and called. Vickers dropped out and the raise came around to Pomeroy. He scowled fearfully at his cards.

"I've only got a pair of jacks, my openers, but I always win the first pot, so—I'll just have to call that—and kick it up five hundred, Mr. Blake."

Chapman skinned his cards again, although he knew very well that he had merely a pair of fours. Then he nodded. Castlemon, at his right, sighed and tossed in his cards.

Chapman counted out five blues and put five more with them. "My dad always told me to call every bet."

Faced with the necessity of adding another thousand dollars to what he had already invested in an uncertain pot, Sutton threw in his hand.

Pomeroy called Chapman. "So you *are* a gold miner," he remarked.

He called for three cards. Sutton glanced inquiringly at Chapman. He smiled. "I like the cards I've got."

Pomeroy exclaimed. "On the first hand?"

"I might not get them again all evening. That's the way it goes. You opened, Mr. Pomeroy."

Pomeroy looked at his cards. "To tell you the truth, I caught another jack. But—I'm not going to bet them."

Chapman counted his chips, thirteen hundred and seventy-five dollars' worth. He shoved them to the center of the table. "My table stakes, Mr. Pomeroy."

Pomeroy moistened his lips with the tip of his tongue. "You really mean that?"

"I'm afraid I do."

Pomeroy shook his head. "We're gentlemen, Mr. Blake, but I'm going to ask an ungentlemanly favor—to satisfy my unnatural curiosity—even if I don't call you, will you show me your hand?"

"Whoa!" exclaimed Alan Vickers. "You can't do that, Elton!"

Pomeroy twisted his face comically. "You want me to lose sleep for weeks worrying about whether or not I got bluffed?"

"Don't show him, Blake," said Castlemon. "He's foreclosed on so many people, he ought to pay for any favor that's given *him*."

"Ah," said Chapman, "you're a banker, Mr. Pomeroy. In that case . . . I'll show you. If you don't call."

Pomeroy looked at his cards once more to assure himself that he couldn't squeeze out a fourth jack. Then he tossed them down. "All right, you win."

Chapman spread out his cards, face up.

Pomeroy's face flooded with hot blood. "Why, damn you, Mr. Blake!"

The others exclaimed to cover up Pomeroy's thinly veiled insult. "He's bluffed a banker!" cried Sutton.

Alan Vickers shook his head in admiration. "You have the face for it, Blake. I was convinced you had a straight at the very least."

"I figured four of a kind," Castlemon said. "Come now, Pomeroy, what did you think he had?"

Pomeroy forced a belated laugh, but his lips were still twitching. "A full house . . . at least. . . ."

That was the biggest pot for an hour. Chapman didn't try another bluff, for he knew that he would be called. He played his cards closely. They were good players, all of the others, particularly Castlemon. Chapman had expected that. Any man who could risk a thousand dollars in the wheat pit on the gesture of a thumb had to be a good poker player. Vickers, too, played a stiff game, betting them when he had them. His only weakness was, as Castlemon had told Chapman earlier, a bad habit of drawing to inside straights. Those foolish ventures kept Vickers' stack of chips down.

Sutton played well, but drew bad cards. Pomeroy got fairly good hands, but bet recklessly at times, trying to recoup his early losses. As a result, he soon had to buy a new stack of chips, giving Vickers his check for them.

Chapman won a little more during the first hour of play and in the second hour won two rather large pots, which brought his total winnings up to nearly four thousand dollars. They had a round of drinks then and Wilton, the butler, brought sandwiches.

Chapman lost a thousand dollars during the next hour and when they decided to quit was three thousand dollars ahead. With their coats already on to leave, Pomeroy, who was the heaviest loser, irritably asked the others to cut high card for a thousand dollars.

Vickers demurred. "You know I don't like cutting, Elton."

"You're ahead, aren't you?" Pomeroy snapped irritably.

Vickers glowered at Pomeroy. "All right, then, count me in."

Sutton, who had the alibi of having lost money, refused. Castlemon, however, put in his thousand dollars and Chapman, as the big winner, naturally put up his own.

Pomeroy shuffled the cards quickly and slapped the deck down for Chapman to make the first cut. Chapman took hold of the deck and a little ripple ran through him as his sensitive fingers felt the roughened card. Someone—Pomeroy, undoubtedly, since he had forced the cut on the others—had raked the card with his finger nail. It was three fourths of the way down the pack, so the first cutters would naturally not cut it.

Chapman hesitated. Then he picked up the top part of the deck, all the way down to the roughed card. He apologized instantly. "Gosh, I took most of the deck!"

Pomeroy's eyes were glaring at him. The others cut easily leaving a few cards for Pomeroy. The banker was black in the face by that time.

Chapman turned up his cards. "Ace," he said, without looking down.

"You are lucky tonight," said Castlemon turning up a four. Vickers showed a ten spot and Pomeroy, exposing his card last, turned up a king with an exclamation of disgust.

Vickers' butler had summoned two hansom cabs, since Sutton and Pomeroy were going direct to their homes on the north side and the others were going downtown.

At the last moment, when they were at the door, Vickers said, "Say, I almost forgot. I promised to look in at the office before turning in. The boys are working on a small case. . . . Mind if I ride down with you, Castlemon?"

"Not at all. Hop in."

Chapman had half suspected that Vickers was not going to let him walk out of the house.

As they rode across the bridge into the loop, Vickers said, "Pomeroy's a poor loser. I don't think I'll invite him up to play, any more."

Castlemon chuckled. "Take him once or twice more and he'll be absconding with the bank's money. . . . I think I'll change my account to the Wheat Exchange tomorrow."

Vickers chuckled. "Are you staying long in Chicago, Mr. Blake?"

"No," Chapman replied. "I'm planning to go on to New York."

"I'm sorry to hear that, Blake," said Castlemon. "I was hoping to get you interested in a wheat deal or two. Things are going to pick up in a few days."

"Oh, I'm not going to stay in New York. I'm coming back this way. In fact, I was sort of counting on what you promised me earlier in the evening—to take me down tomorrow for a little flier."

"Fine! Maybe you can double that money you won tonight."

"Something on, Phil?" Vickers asked. "Count me in for a piece of it."

"Sure, why not?"

The hanson cab pulled up at the hotel and the three men climbed out.

"How about a nightcap?" Vickers suggested.

"A good idea," Chapman agreed.

Castlemon was willing and they entered the hotel and moved toward the saloon door. As they approached it, Chapman exclaimed: "I'll join you in a second! I just want to ask at the desk if the jeweler left my watch. . . ."

He turned and without looking back, walked toward the desk. He wondered if Vickers was waiting at the door of the saloon, to watch him, but he forced himself to keep his eyes straight ahead and deliberately went past the desk to a door, opening on Monroe Street. He went through.

Vickers did not call to him.

He stepped down from the sidewalk on Monroe, crossed the street and turned the corner on State Street. He quickened his pace, then.

It was flight, again. But this time Chapman was wearing a gentleman's Prince Albert, broadcloth trousers and white ruffled shirt. He was a conspicuous person to be traveling afar from a city. Especially in a country that he did not know.

He had no alternative.

He walked steadily west and northward, through the darkened streets and after a while came to the river. He recalled then the muskrat trapper on Goose Island and, grinning crookedly, made his way toward the tiny shack made from old packing boxes and driftwood washed ashore by the river.

The trapper was asleep, rolled up in torn blankets, but Chapman roused him. He was astonished when he recognized Chapman.

"Why, Mr. Blake, what're you doin' here at this time o' night?"

"I'm in a little trouble," Chapman exclaimed. "A bit of a fight. The man's got friends and—well, I've got to get away in a hurry. Look—what's the best and quickest way to get West . . . if you don't want to be seen?"

The trapper gestured to the river. "That way, Mr. Blake. Swiggins, a friend o' mine, will take you in a canoe. He'll take you as far he can go, then you can cross to the Illinois River and float down to the Missipp'."

"Fine. You can keep your mouth shut? Yes—of course." Chapman took bills from his pocket. "Here's two hundred dollars."

The trapper gasped. "Why, that's more'n I make in a year trappin' 'rats!"

"All right. I need some clothes. These are too conspicuous."

The trapper's face fell. "All I got besides those I wear is an old pair of britches and a shirt that's pretty far gone—"

"They'll do." Chapman began peeling off his Prince Albert. The flowered vest followed, then the cartridge belt and Navy Colt. The trapper looked at the big gun, but made no comment. A few minutes later Chapman was dressed in the trapper's filthy breeches and flannel shirt. His own sister wouldn't have known him.

A quarter mile up the island, the trapper roused Swiggins, the boatman, and explained Chapman's predicament. Swiggins was quite agreeable and in a few minutes they shoved off.

At Ottawa, the next afternoon, Chapman gave Swiggins some money and sent him into the village to buy a newspaper, some food, and clothing that was not quite as disreputable as what he was wearing.

They got into the canoe again when Swiggins returned.

Kneeling in the bow Chapman perused the copy of the Chicago *Tribune* that Swiggins had purchased for him. He was vaguely disappointed not to find mention of himself in the paper. He might have found some clue as to Vickers' intentions in a statement, but it was missing. On an inside page, however, he found something else of interest. It was a brief statement, sent to the paper by telegraph from St. Louis.

BANK ROBBER ATTEMPTS ESCAPE, IS KILLED

Bligh, the bank robber, arrested early this week, was shot and killed today by Sheriff Gregg of Clay County. Sheriff Gregg, who had come from Clay County with extradition papers, was returning with his prisoner, when Bligh, according to Sheriff Gregg's statement, made a desperate effort to escape. He plunged from a moving train. Keen disappointment was expressed in the prisoner's death, for it had been hoped that he would implicate the other members of the band which have terrorized the banks of the state. . . .

Chapman tore the paper across and dropped it into the water. Poor, foolish Bligh; he had redeemed himself for his recklessness. In Clay County they would have done things to Billy. He would have told the names of his companions— not that they weren't known already—but they could, backed by a signed statement, have been used as proof. Rather than give his friends away, Billy had taken the desperate way out.

Ten

THREE MONTHS BEFORE, Abilene, Kansas, had been a hamlet of a dozen mud-roofed huts spread over a half mile of prairie. The Kansas Pacific Railroad, building through, had considered Abilene of such little importance that it had disdained to put up a railroad station at the point, despite the fact that Abilene was the county seat of Dickinson County.

In August, Joseph McCoy, an Illinois man with vision, had selected Abilene as the logical point on the railroad to which Texas cattle should be brought for shipping to the eastern markets. He had so much faith in his judgment that he built at his own expense shipping yards that would have been large for a town one thousand times the size of Abilene. He also began construction of an elaborate hotel for the expected drovers. Not content, then, to wait for wandering herds the same visionary sent scouts down into the Indian territory to locate them and persuade the drovers to come to Abilene.

The first herd arrived in September. Overnight, Abilene became a boom town, the first city of the Kansas plains. Where they came from then, no one knew, but suddenly they descended upon Abilene in hordes; saloon men, gamblers, prostitutes, storekeepers, and all the parasites without which no boom town seems to thrive.

The drovers came too, and with them hordes of lean, tanned Texas cowboys, who had driven the herds up from the Texas plains. They were wild men, the cowboys. They had spent weeks on the lonely trail, living on a diet of fresh beef and coffee made from muddy, stagnant water.

Chapman rode into Abilene at high noon, a time that should have been the quietest part of the day. He found Abilene running at full blast. There was only a short street of false fronted buildings, facing the railroad tracks, but at least a hundred cow ponies were tied at the hitch rails. The strip of earth between the rails and the buildings, that served in place of sidewalks, was jammed with moving humanity.

He found a place for his horse in front of the Cattleman's Barber Shop and went inside. He had to wait a half hour

before one of the four barbers was free. He got a haircut and
a shave then, instructing the barber to leave the week's old
mustache on his upper lip. Glancing in the mirror as he paid
he scarcely recognized himself. He had put on weight these
last few weeks and the pallor had gone from his skin. The
mustache made him look several years older. Which reminded
him that he had passed his twenty-first birthday.

He got his horse at the hitch rail and led it to the big livery
stable at the end of the street. Then he walked back to the
largest building in the block, a two-story frame building, over
which was a newly painted sign: *Cattle Drivers' Hotel & Bar*.
The building was unpainted and being made of green lumber
would shrink and have half inch cracks after a few weeks.

He went inside. There was a tiny lobby with a counter, over
which was a small sign: *Rooms*. And a pimply-faced stripling
on guard.

"I'd like a room," Chapman said to the youth.

"Day, week, or month?"

"How much is it by the day?"

"Five dollars."

Chapman grunted. "I said, day."

"That's right, five dollars a day. Thirty a week. And you
better rent it now, because we're always sold out by
suppertime."

"All right. I'll take it for a week. Give me the key."

"There ain't no key. There's a bolt on the inside. Lock
it when you go to sleep. Number 4, at the head of the stairs.
What's your name?"

"James Castlemon." Chapman's mouth twitched as he
gave the name of his recent acquaintance in Chicago. There
was no chance of the city-bred wheat speculator coming out
here to the frontier.

The youth wrote in a ledger, then straightened and got
ready for a friendly chat. "Drover, Mr. Castlemon? Maybe
you're looking for some fun, huh?"

"Perhaps."

"Why don't you go over to the Bull's Head? Two doors
up the street. The whisky's the best in town. . . ."

Chapman nodded to the bar, opening off the lobby to the
left. "You have a bar here."

"Sure, if it's just liquor you want. We ain't got no gals,
here. Boss won't allow it. But you go over to the Bull's
Head and ask for Tessie. Tell her I sent you—"

"Lester!"

The pimply clerk winced and turning quickly pretended to be looking for something on a littered table behind the counter.

A woman came down the stairs and nodded coolly to Chapman. "How do you do, sir," she said, "I am Mrs. Vivian Braddock, the landlady."

Chapman scarcely controlled a blink of surprise. Mrs. Braddock was certainly no more than twenty-two and looked even younger than that. She was rather tall and slender, with clear, slightly tanned complexion, and hair the color of burnished copper. It was piled high on her head, with a coil nestling on the nape of her neck.

She wore a dark-green velvet dress, with a white collar and cuffs.

Chapman swept off his hat and bowed. "How do you do, Madam. I—my name is Castlemon. I've just registered, to stay for a time."

"We're glad to have you with us," Mrs. Braddock said in a dignified tone. "I hope, however, that you do not get the wrong impression. We most certainly are not steerers for the Bull's Head, regardless—" she glanced severely at her youthful clerk—"of any impression our employees may create."

Chapman smiled. "I understand, Mrs. Braddock. Thank you."

Mrs. Braddock nodded. "If it is—refreshments, my husband will be glad to serve you in the barroom."

Chapman bowed again and turned to the barroom. He looked with interest at the two bartenders behind the long bar that ran down one side of the room and wondered which of the two was Mr. Braddock.

One was bald and over fifty, the other was considerably younger, but weighed well over two hundred pounds. Chapman decided that the fat man was the husband and then a lean, sardonic-eyed man leaning against the front of the bar, spoke to him.

"How do you do, stranger. I'm Wes Braddock, the proprietor. Will you honor me by having a drink with me?"

He was about thirty, dressed in a black Prince Albert and stovepipe hat. His hands were long and soft, betraying his real vocation—gambling.

Chapman introduced himself by his new name. "Yes, I'll be glad to drink with you, sir."

A bartender brought whisky and glasses. Braddock tossed

off his glass in a single gulp and immediately filled it again. He looked pointedly at Chapman's glass, but the latter smiled and showed that it was still half filled.

"Just up from Texas?" Braddock asked.

"Yes, but I didn't bring a herd. I'm here merely to size up the situation. This is all so new. . . ."

"You're telling me! But it's the biggest thing the West ever saw. Would you believe that a thousand cars of steers have already gone out of Abilene? In a single month. Why, next year there'll be a half million head of cattle come to this town. And there'll be buyers here from as far east as Pittsburgh."

Chapman nodded. "They need this beef. But the question is, how much of this beef can the East absorb?"

"A million head!" declared Braddock. "And there'll be at least half that many come to this town next year. Joe McCoy sure started something when he located his shipping pens here. But it'll be the first herds that bring the best prices; steers that have been fattened over the winter right here at Abilene."

"You mean," said Chapman, "that some of the drovers are going to hold their herds here all winter?"

"The farsighted ones. The steers get pretty thin on the trip up here and the buyers are not too keen to pay high prices for them. But they're offering a premium for good, fat steers. I don't mind telling you that I'm doing a little speculating myself. I've bought me a thousand steers right now and I'm going to fatten them right here at Abilene and sell them to the first buyers that come along in spring. I only wish I could afford to buy another thousand head. There's a drover here with a herd—" He stopped and twirled his empty glass. "I'm sorry, I let my enthusiasm run away with me. . . ."

"Not at all," said Chapman. "That's why I'm in Abilene, to size up the cattle business. Frankly, I'm interested in making a profit on cattle and—" He hedged.

Braddock reached out and caught Chapman's arm. "Then, sir, let me give you a tip. Since I'm strapped myself, I can't avail myself of it and I may as well pass it on. Mose Hendricks is the man to see. He's staying right here at the hotel and he's got the finest herd you ever laid your eyes on. A little thin right now as is to be expected after their long journey, but all choice, big steers that'll double in value over the winter."

"I'd like to meet Mr. Hendricks some time."

"You shall!" exclaimed Braddock. "And right now. He went up to his room only fifteen minutes ago, to take a nap. I'll go—"

"No hurry, Mr. Braddock. I've just got here and—"

"It's no trouble. He'll be glad to talk to you. I'll get him." Braddock hurried out of the saloon.

Chapman drank the rest of his whisky and scowled at the empty glass. There must be something about him that inspired the confidence of glib salesmen. He'd had no intention whatever of getting into anything like this and it had been only too apparent to him that Braddock was angling for a commission on a deal, yet he'd encouraged the man and now he was in for it. Well, the best he could do was buy a round or two of drinks and evade the issue as best he could.

"Mr. Castlemon," exclaimed Braddock, returning. "I want you to shake the hand of my friend, Mose Hendricks. . . ."

Chapman turned from the bar and held out his hand to Clem Tancred; big Clem Tancred with a beard. "It's a pleasure, Mr. Hen—" he began and then Clem roared: "Jim, you son of a gun!"

Wes Braddock's eyes darted from Chapman to Tancred. "Say . . . you gentlemen know each other?"

Clem gripped Chapman's hand in a grip of iron and pounded his back with his free hand. "Cripes, Jim, how'd you know I was here?"

"I didn't," said Chapman, shaking his head. "I didn't dream I'd run into you here. I thought you'd be down in Texas by now. . . ."

Clem Tancred chuckled. Then he put his left hand under Braddock's arm and his right under Chapman's. He led them away from the bar.

"Braddock," he said in a hoarse whisper. "This is Jim Chapman. . . ."

Braddock inhaled softly. "And I took you for a cattle drover! I must be getting simple-minded. And you led me on. What the devil was the idea, Chapman?"

"I was interested. After all, if there's money to be made in cattle—"

"Huh!" cried Clem. "You mean you still got some money left, Jim?"

Chapman shrugged. "More than I had before. I had a bit of . . . luck."

"What? You pulled a job by yourself?"

Chapman looked so steadily at Clem Tancred that the big man flushed. "It's all right, Jim; Braddock knows. Matter of fact, we're together in a little business here."

"Cattle business," Braddock corrected. "And we really do have a herd. All we need is some additional capital to carry it over the winter."

Chapman glanced at Clem for verification. Clem nodded. "Dan and me bought the herd—Dan's out with it now. Gosh, he'll be glad to see you. We didn't have quite enough money to swing the deal, so we cut Braddock in on it. We stand to make a pile of money in the spring—if we can raise five thousand somewhere to feed the stock over the winter. We got to buy hay—and some corn."

"I've got five thousand dollars."

"Whew!" sighed Clem Tancred in relief. "I was afraid we'd have to, uh . . . I mean I was afraid we'd lose the herd."

"When do you need the money?"

"Right now," said Braddock. "The grass is pretty near gone and if we want to get any hay without having to haul it a hundred miles we'll have to buy it now. We'll need at least a thousand tons. . . ."

Chapman dug into his pockets and brought out two fat rolls. He counted off the money and put the rest away. Braddock's eyes followed the remainder of the money to Chapman's pocket.

Chapman shoved the money to Clem.

"You're in for a third, Jim," Clem said. "Me and Dan have a third together and Braddock has a third. The herd cost us just under ten thousand. We'll sell it for thirty in the spring."

"Perhaps a little more," said Braddock. "Shall I see Schneider about that hay? . . ."

Eleven

TANCRED TOSSED the money to Braddock. "Might as well. He promised he wouldn't sell to anyone else for a couple of days, but you can't trust a Dutchman. . . ."

"You can't," said Braddock, getting up. "I'm glad you came to Abilene, Chapman. We may work out some interesting propositions. . . ." He walked out of the saloon.

"Great chap, Braddock," said Clem.

Chapman looked thoughtfully at Clem for a moment. Then he said suddenly, "Have you heard about Billy Bligh?"

Clem's eyes remained blank. "No. He left us in Iowa to go to St. Louis. . . . What? . . ."

"He's dead. He went to St. Louis and talked too much . . . to strangers."

Clem exclaimed, then suddenly his face turned red. "You mean . . . Braddock?"

Chapman nodded.

"But it's all right—here, Jim. This is Kansas. Hell, there's no law out here. Two men were killed on the street yesterday. There isn't an evening someone doesn't get shot. This is Hell, with the lid off.' And Braddock—Braddock's the hottest man in this town."

"I met his wife a few minutes ago. Is she aware . . . of her husband's character?"

Clem shrugged. "She's a honey, isn't she? But don't be fooled by her looks, Jim. She's plenty hard. As far as I know she thinks my name is Hendricks, but—" Clem shrugged. "How did he die—Billy?"

"Gregg. He came to St. Louis for Billy after he was arrested. Billy tried to escape. That's what the paper said."

Clem's face darkened. "You think maybe Billy didn't try to escape. Why, the dirty—"

"I'd rather think Billy did try to escape. I think he deliberately took the chance of being killed, rather than be made to implicate us. Clem . . . are you fully aware of just what we did?"

"I think I am. What was so terrible about it? We did a lot worse during the war."

"That *was* war, Clem. The Richfield thing—and the Freedom one—wasn't war. Alan Vickers is after us."

"That black son of a bitch!"

Chapman laughed shortly, hollowly. "Clem, I never told you that I know Alan Vickers. I met him on the train—the day I was returning to Freedom—when I kicked Pike off the train. Vickers offered me a job. As a detective, Clem!"

Clem Tancred gasped. "You . . . a Vickers man?"

"It *is* funny, isn't it? Vickers was pretty insistent about it, too. I—I told him I was a former Confederate and he seemed to think that was all right since he was opening a new office in Kansas City."

"Be damned. Why—that'd be the office that's now on the Richfield and Freedom jobs! Christ, what would old Alan say if he knew. . . ."

"He does know, Clem. That's what I've been working up to. You see, I ran into Vickers again. In Chicago." Rapidly, he told Clem about the Chicago episode. The big man chortled in high glee when Chapman related the account of the poker game, but when he came to the point of his sudden flight from the hotel, he shook his head.

"But you don't know for sure if Vickers remembered you. He might have not have placed you at all."

"Oh, he did, Clem. I know. I've read the Chicago papers almost every day since and there hasn't been another word in them about the whole business—not even about Billy Bligh."

"Why should there be? That happened in Missouri. . . ."

Chapman sighed. "You don't realize, Clem, that those two stories—the Freedom affair and the Richfield one—were two of the greatest newspaper stories since Appomattox. Why, I read about the Freedom job in New York City. They played it up for days. It was the first time in all the world that a bank had been held up by armed men in broad daylight."

Clem Tancred's eyes widened. "Is that so, Jim? I didn't know. . . . Then, why isn't there anything about it in the papers now?"

"Because Vickers has silenced it. He's working on the case and doesn't want his hand tipped."

"I don't get it? How can Vickers silence the newspapers?"

"Look, Clem," said Chapman. "You and I and the rest of the boys know the name of Vickers merely because he was mentioned a lot during the war for his spy work. But did you

know that all during the war Vickers still operated his detective agency? That he has branch offices throughout the
country and is paid huge fees by the railroads? I was at his
house in Chicago. It's the house of a millionaire. We've been
underestimating Vickers. He's one of the most important men
in this country. . . ."

'Mebbe so," Clem admitted grudgingly, "but he didn't do
much around Freedom. We never even saw his face there."

"Freedom is something else again, Clem. Freedom is under
the control of the Union Army—but that control is pretty
slender. The army knows as well as does everyone else, that
seventy-five per cent of the people in western Missouri are
Southern in sympathy and that they would do anything to
protect another Southerner against the North—the north
meaning The Law, in this case. Vickers would have to move
pretty slow in our section. I wouldn't be a bit surprised if
Sheriff Gregg and George Pike weren't drawing money from
Alan Vickers. Maybe Vickers figured the best way to clean
up the mess was to have the bank robbers killed in what
appeared to be a local squabble."

Anger distorted Clem's big face. "I've got a good notion
to take the cars back to Freedom and clean up on Gregg
and Pike."

"Not for a while, yet, Clem. Let the thing simmer down.
Maybe in spring. Are you in touch with Freedom?"

"No. There's no one there now that I give damn about.
Some cousins, but the less I see of them the better off I
am. How about you?"

"Not a word. I haven't dared write my sister for fear they'd
open her mail. I'd like to know what's going on, though. Is
it possible to get a Kansas City paper here?"

"Oh sure. A bundle of them come in every day. Been too
busy myself to read them. Braddock gets them regular. . . ."

"Speaking of Braddock, Clem," said Chapman, frowning.
"I wish you hadn't told him about yourself . . . and me."

"I didn't. Well, not until last week. We were here two
weeks and he'd told me he served in the 19th Alabama
under Leonidas Polk and we found out we knew a lot of
different officers and one thing led to another. . . . Well, he's
a pretty shrewd fellow, Jim. He finally came right out and
asked me if I was on the dodge and knowing that he was
cutting things pretty sharp here himself—"

"How do you mean, sharp?"

Clem laughed. "You ought to see him with a pack of

cards. He's got a faro layout that's a whiz. And I never saw a Mex that could play three-card monte the way he does. . . ."

"A crooked gambler," Chapman said softly. He looked up suddenly. The pimply-faced hotel clerk, Lester, had approached the table without Chapman hearing him.

He said, "Uh, Mr. Castlemon, the boss says she'd like to talk to you if you ain't busy."

"Mrs. Braddock?"

Chapman looked blankly at Clem Tancred, then got up. "I'll be back, Clem."

He followed Lester to the lobby. The clerk pointed to a door that was just beside the counter. "She's in the office."

Chapman opened the door. He saw a small room about ten by twelve, furnished roughly with a scrubbed table, an armchair and a sofa. Mrs. Braddock was sitting in the armchair.

She smiled at Chapman and nodded to the sofa. "Won't you have a seat?"

Chapman sat down on the sofa and Mrs. Braddock turned her chair partly to face him. "Mr. Castlemon," she began, "I understand you gave my husband some money."

"No," he said, "I gave some money to an old friend I discovered was here. Mr. Hendricks. I believe Mr. Hendricks is a partner in a business venture with your husband."

"Well," she said, "that's a roundabout way of putting it, but we won't quibble. It amounts to the same. My husband got the money."

"He's buying some hay with it."

She smiled thinly, then she reached to the table and picked up a folded newspaper. "This is the Kansas City Star. It just came in this afternoon on the train. Would you care to see it?"

He leaned forward and took the paper. It was folded so that his eyes fell on a two-column head.

ARREST IN FREEDOM AND RICHFIELD BANK ROBBERIES
Ed Taylor Arrested for Bank Holdup. Warrant Served by Sheriff Gregg. Authorities Closing in on Gang. Seek Clem and Dan Tancred, Clark Welker and Jim Chapman, Former Bushwhackers.

He didn't read the rest of the story. He tapped the paper lightly. "You know?"

"My husband told me that Mr. Hendricks is Clem Tancred. You—"

"Chapman. Ed Taylor is my brother-in-law. He had nothing to do with this."

"Can he raise ten thousand dollars bail?"

Chapman's mouth became a thin, straight line. "Ed hasn't got fifty dollars. But . . . I'm afraid I'll have to get that money back from Brad—your husband."

She shook her head. "Wes Braddock never gave a sucker back a dollar in his life."

He looked at her stony-eyed. "Sucker?"

"It's not a nice word, is it? But you are a sucker, you know. And so is your friend, Clem Tancred. Wes didn't own that herd. It's owned by a Texan who'll be showing up here any day. He preferred to come to Kansas by way of Galveston, New Orleans and the river, rather than overland. Hudkins—the man Tancred took to be the owner—is merely the trail boss of the herd."

"Well," said Chapman, "I think I'll go and see Hudkins."

"No," she said. "Don't. Hudkins is a killer."

For a long moment, Chapman looked at Mrs. Braddock. Then he tilted his head sidewards. "Why do you tell me this?"

"Because in another week, Abilene will roll over and die. The season's finished. Wes knew it and he'd been trying to gather—to put it bluntly—getaway money, for several weeks. He walked out of this hotel a few minutes ago with the money you gave him . . . and every dollar out of the safe. He stepped on to the westbound train and neither you nor I will ever see him again."

Chapman whistled softly. "You don't seem greatly concerned?"

She laughed shortly. "For the past year our relationship had been that of business partners. I ran the hotel and Braddock the—the saloon and gambling. He was a gambler on the Mississippi River steamers before the war."

"And you?"

She looked at him steadily. "My father ran a tavern in Aubrey, Kansas."

"In '62?"

She nodded. "I saw him killed. It was a guerrilla with a pirate's beard. A man with yellow eyeballs."

"Anderson, Bloody Bill. I—I rode with Anderson."

"I know."

There was nothing more he could say. By all the rules she should be a mortal enemy of Jim Chapman. But she wasn't. There was nothing hostile in her attitude.

He got up from the sofa. "You'll be leaving here, then?"

"Why? This is as good a place as any to spend the winter. And next spring—well, the drovers may come back."

He left her and went back to the saloon. "Let's take a little ride, Clem," he told his friend.

Clem got up quickly from the table. He had been drinking during Chapman's absence and was a little unsteady on his feet. Outside, they walked to the livery stable. But it wasn't until they were in the saddle that Chapman asked the whereabouts of Hudkins' herd.

"It's about three miles west of town," Clem replied. "But what's the use going out there now? Braddock won't be there. He's up north buying that hay."

"Braddock took the westbound train," Chapman said curtly. "He took with him my five thousand dollars and whatever money he got from you and Dan. He doesn't own that herd, and neither does Hudkins."

The expression that came to Clem Tancred's broad face was almost ludicrous. "What are you talking about, Jim?"

"Mrs. Braddock told me. He walked out on her. You've— we—have been bilged."

Clem Tancred kicked his horse in the belly. The animal sprang forward. "Come on, Jim!" he yelled over his shoulder.

Hudkins saw them coming from a distance and it may have been mere coincidence that eight or ten of his men were gathered about him when they rode up.

Dan Tancred went popeyed when he saw Chapman. The latter merely nodded to him and addressed the red-bearded, fishy-eyed man who appeared to be the leader of the cowboys.

"Hudkins," he said, "your partner has skipped. I gave him five thousand dollars to buy hay for this herd."

"Why," said Hudkins innocently, "why would you do that? Mr. Simpson'll be here any day now, and I don't reckon he figures on wintering the stock here. Fact is, he's figgerin' on sellin'."

"Hudkins!" roared Clem Tancred, "reach for your gun!"

Hudkins bared his teeth. "What's the idea? I give your brother a job an'—" he half turned and appealed to the cowboys—"what do you make of this, boys?"

The "boys" expressed their opinions by an assorted batch of curses and muttered imprecations about "goddam Yanks."

Jim Chapman held up his hand. "Hudkins, I want all the money you've got."

"A holdup!" cried Hudkins. "Hear that, boys?"

Chapman scarcely seemed to move, but suddenly his long-barreled Navy Colt was in his hand, pointing down at Hudkins. He spoke to Dan, "Go through him. Then take a look through his equipment. The rest of you . . ."

By that time Clem Tancred was down from his horse, gun in hand and stalking forward. He passed within a couple of feet of Hudkins and wheeling suddenly lashed out with the barrel of his Colt. It rapped Hudkins along the side of the head and the herd foreman toppled to the ground.

A sudden hush fell upon the cowboys. They looked at one another, but lacked a leader—and a signal. They sensed that Chapman and the Tancreds were not men to bluff easily.

Dan Tancred went through Hudkins' clothes and dumped a handful of silver on the ground. Search of the chuck wagon and camp equipment produced a small bag of silver dollars, not more than two hundred.

When the loot was heaped on the ground, Chapman swore softly. "Braddock bilked him, too. The dirty—!"

The Tancreds agreed with that comment and added their own lurid adjectives. Clem began to scoop up the money, but Chapman stopped him. "That change won't help any."

Hudkins was beginning to stir when the trio was mounted again. Chapman turned in his saddle for a last word to the cowboys. "Tell Hudkins that Braddock took the westbound train. Maybe he can catch up with him."

Then they galloped off. But not toward Abilene. There was no use going there, now. The game was played out.

Twelve

EVELYN COMSTOCK had been born in Johnson County, Missouri. Her father was a large planter, employing many slaves, but as Evelyn grew up, her father, because of his investments, began spending more and more time in town. When she was ten, the plantation was run by an overseer.

Major Comstock was the wealthiest man in the community. When the local bank failed, he reopened it and continued it with his private capital.

She was twelve when the world began to fall about them. Major Comstock saw it coming and wisely prepared for it—from a financial viewpoint. He withdrew more and more of his capital and transferred it to St. Louis and Chicago. But he was a Kentuckian by birth and his sympathies were naturally with the South, although he did not believe that the differences between the two sections were sufficient to make a recourse to arms necessary.

War came. To Missouri it came like a thunderbolt. Evelyn's brother, Cliff, six years older, enlisted in one of the militia companies that were formed. Soon he was off, fighting at Wilson's Creek, against the Federal forces. Victorious, the Confederacy swept western Missouri. It was but the prelude to the holocaust. The Confederacy receded and in its wake came the Terror.

Unionists and those who called themselves Southerners ravaged the countryside. Evelyn was fourteen when the devastation that was Order Number 11 came to Johnson County. It meant complete evacuation imposed on the citizenry by the Union Army. All day long Evelyn saw the pillars of smoke that indicated Southern homes going up. She was alone at home with her mother, when the soldiers came and put the torch to their own home. By that time her father had already been one year with the Confederate Army. Evelyn helped to load a few belongings into a farm wagon and with her mother traveled to Nebraska. The weeks that followed were a nightmare and when they were over, her mother was gone.

In the end, her father and brother both returned miraculously. They never went to Johnson County again. They settled in Clay County, in the village of Freedom. Her father began to rebuild his fortune, drawing upon the money he had held all during the years in Chicago and St. Louis.

Life was gradually beginning anew for all of them. At eighteen she met Martin Halliday, the brilliant young attorney who, folks said, would go far.

Sometimes she wondered if she was in love with him. When he was not with her, she thought of him, and even longed for his companionship. And when he came, she was vaguely unsatisfied.

He was everything that a girl could ask for. Tall, handsome, in his late twenties. Brilliant in his chosen profession. A captain in the late Confederate cavalry he got along well even with the Union authorities. He was intelligent and a brilliant conversationalist. Only—he was cold.

He had never actually proposed to her, but somehow that seemed to be taken for granted and Martin talked of the future, when they would be married. Had he pressed her, she would probably have agreed to an early marriage, for she was lonesome in Freedom.

Things were like that, when Evelyn took the trip to St. Louis, to visit her cousin, Jean. On her return occurred the incident of the drunken ruffian, Pike, and the intercession on her behalf of the pale youth, with the bitter look in his eyes.

She hadn't planned on going to the dance at Funk's Grove. Well, they had expected to go and then Martin had been compelled to go to Kansas City on business. Normally, Evelyn would have remained at home.

At the last minute, she persuaded her brother to take her to the dance. "Martin won't like it," Cliff said sardonically, "but it'll do him some good. And as for me—well, I'd like to get a little better acquainted with that little Yankee girl, Bea Wainright."

They went to the dance and big Clem Tancred asked her to dance. "First time I've been able to get you away from Halliday," Clem chuckled as he danced her clumsily about the uneven floor.

"He'll be back tomorrow," Evelyn retorted. "But tell me about your friend—the prodigal Jim Chapman. Has he told you that he did me a good turn today?"

"Jim?" exclaimed Clem. "He hasn't even said he knew you. He was always like that. A clam."

"I wouldn't call him that," Evelyn said. "I think, perhaps, he's seen a little too much."

"He has," Clem agreed. "And it made too much of an impression on him. Me—it didn't affect me much. Jim got in too young and he stuck to it too long. It's going to take him a long time to come back."

That night Evelyn thought of Jim Chapman. She saw his lean face and haunting eyes as she drifted into sleep.

In the morning, she awoke, sober—and worried.

Martin would be back today. In the evening he would come to see her and tell about his Kansas City trip. He would go into great detail about it all, and Evelyn would scarcely hear him. Yes, she *would* tonight. She would concentrate, for if she didn't she would think of Jim Chapman. And she didn't want to think about him.

She decided to keep busy that day and shortly after breakfast put on a gingham dress and sunbonnet and went out to work in her garden.

It was no use. Her hands worked automatically, but her mind was far away. After a while she looked up . . . and there he was. Pale and more haunted of face than ever.

He moved toward her and fell.

What she did afterwards was instinctive. She had Rupe, the colored handyman, carry him into the carriage shed. Then she dispatched Rupe to Jim's sister and when he returned with the alarming news of all that had happened that morning, she got him into the wagon.

She went through the next week as if in a daze. She saw Martin Halliday, talked with him and scarcely remembered afterwards of what they had talked. Her brother, noting her condition, declared that she needed a trip and since he was going to Richfield on business for a couple of days, he would take her along. Evelyn grasped at the opportunity.

She saw Jim Chapman again, saw him with a smoking revolver.

Afterwards, when they were driving back to Freedom, her brother was silent for a long while, but finally he said, without looking at her, "It *is* Jim Chapman, then?"

And then Evelyn admitted to her brother, what she had been fighting within herself for days. "I'm afraid it is, but what can I do about it, Cliff? You know . . . what he is."

Soberly her brother said, "Rupe told me. Thought I ought to know. I didn't say anything to you, Evelyn. I'd hoped you'd forget."

"I can't. I've tried and I can't. I'm not in love with him, I'm pretty sure of that. But his face haunts me. It's so bitter. As if he'd looked into . . . hell."

Her brother patted her hand. "I'm sorry, Evelyn. The war's been over two years. He's gone—too far to come back. You'll have to forget him."

She didn't forget him. She saw his face the evening before Martin Halliday came to her with the astonishing letter —the letter containing three thousand dollars in currency.

"What does he think I am, this fellow?" Halliday demanded. "It would ruin me to defend a man like him."

"Why, Martin? Isn't it an attorney's duty to defend those in trouble?"

"Yes, of course. But this Chapman—he's become too infamous. Holding up banks in broad daylight. There's no chance in the world of getting an acquittal for him, if he came to trial."

"But a man like him doesn't find it easy to get an attorney. If he wants to surrender, he should be given a fair chance."

Martin Halliday stared at her. "Why, Evelyn, you don't even know the man."

"Oh, but I do. He—he did me a good turn on the train coming back from St. Louis." Rapidly she related the incident, finishing with, "A man with such instincts can't be all bad. It was—the war. He was on the wrong side. But weren't *we?*"

"But *he* was a guerrilla!"

"He was a Confederate. He lost a brother in the war. His sister—Mrs. Taylor—is as honest a woman as you'll find. She bore a child during the evacuation. . . ."

Thirteen

JIM CHAPMAN remained in his room at the Missouri House in Kansas City, venturing outside only after dark, for his meals. In mid-afternoon of the second day after he mailed the letter, a porter knocked on the door.

"Gen'man to see you, Mistah Castlemon."

Chapman opened the door and regarded the tall man in the gray Prince Albert. "How do you do, Mr. Halliday," he said.

Halliday came into the room and Chapman closed the door behind him.

Halliday said, "I got your letter, containing the retainer. . . ."

"You're accepting?"

Halliday's eyes surveyed the room, not missing the drawn shades. "Why did you write to me? There are other attorneys in Freedom."

"They're not all Southerners."

"Some of them are. Good men. Frankly . . . I don't want to accept your case."

"It's not my case, Mr. Halliday," Chapman exclaimed. "I want nothing. All I want you to do is look after my brother-in-law, Ed Taylor. He had nothing to do with that—that matter, for which they arrested him."

Halliday's forehead wrinkled. "They have no real case against Taylor. They . . . well, they arrested him merely to smoke you out."

"But Ed's in jail! They'll hold him there for months. Put off the trial; I want Ed released."

Halliday shook his head. "They've set enormous bail. Ten thousand dollars—in cash."

"You can get him out if you put up ten thousand?"

"Why, yes. But—where would I get ten thousand?"

"If that's all that's standing between Ed and his freedom, I'll get the money."

"You have ten thousand dollars?"

"No—but I'll get it."

Halliday exclaimed, "You can't do that. I—I don't want anything to do with this."

70

Chapman looked at him pointedly. "Then why did you come?"

Halliday made an angry gesture. "Because I was a fool. Good lord, man, do you realize that I'd be a party to—to that? I'd know beforehand just how you were going to get that money . . . and I'd be handling it after you got it. I can't do that."

"All right," said Chapman. "I'm sorry."

Halliday took a thick envelope from his pocket and laid it on the cheap dresser. "Your retainer. I—you can count on me to keep your confidence, but I just can't be a party—"

"Yes. I know."

Halliday flushed and suddenly stepped to the door. He said, "Good-bye," and went out.

Swiftly, Chapman got his carpetbag from the closet and began packing his few belongings. Putting on his coat and picking up the carpetbag he stepped to the door. At the moment he touched the knob, knuckles rapped on the other side of the panels.

Startled, Chapman set down the carpetbag. When he straightened the Navy Colt was in his hand. He said, "Yes?"

"Jim," a voice said, "open up. . . ."

He gasped and jerked open the door. Evelyn Comstock, her mouth trembling in a quavering smile, looked at him. "May I come in?"

"Miss Comstock," Chapman said, in a tone of awe. "You shouldn't have . . ." He closed the door behind her.

"Martin was here," she said. "I saw by his face that he'd lost his nerve."

"You know?"

"Of course. He came to me with the letter. Didn't want to come. I practically forced him . . . and then he couldn't go through with it."

"But I don't understand? Why should *you* force him to come here?"

"Why did you write to Martin?" she countered.

Embarrassed, he shook his head. "Why . . . I didn't know of any other lawyers in Freedom. And—he *had* been a Confederate."

"Are those the only reasons you selected Martin?"

He bit his lower lip. "Perhaps not. I . . . I remembered what you'd done for me and I was desperate. I wanted to get Ed out of his jam."

"I know, Anne's hit pretty hard."

"You've seen her? She blames me, of course."

"No, she doesn't blame you at all," Evelyn Comstock said. "She says they didn't give you a chance. You weren't looking for trouble and they brought it to you. I—well, I was there when it began. In a way, I was responsible for Pike's enmity toward you. *He* was behind it."

Chapman nodded. "I never told, but Pike was one of the men who killed Clarence Welker and shot me. They—including Pike—were wearing blue uniforms. Still, if it hadn't been that, it might have been something else."

"The war did things . . . to all of us," Evelyn Comstock said in a low tone.

Something in her tone caused him to look steadily at her. And suddenly an electric shock ran through him. Confused, he said, "Did you come to Kansas City with Martin Halliday?"

"No. I came by carriage from Independence. I was afraid he would weaken at the last moment. He did."

"I can't blame him," Chapman laughed shortly. "He tells me that the only thing'll get my brother-in-law out of jail is ten thousand dollars. I told Halliday I'd get the money."

She gasped. "No! You wouldn't . . . again!"

"How else could I get ten thousand dollars?"

"But *twice!*" she cried. "I—I saw you at Richfield. Your face . . . it was terrible. It's haunted me ever since."

"You prevented your brother from shooting me."

"No. . . . You were going to let him shoot you, rather than stop him. I—I prevented *that*. But . . ."

He took a step toward her, saw that she wasn't going to retreat and that knowledge stopped him. He groaned. "Oh, why did I ever come back to this country? I should have stayed in Mexico."

"Is it too late—to go back?"

"Back where?"

"I don't know. Perhaps to four years ago, before you got into the war. After all, you're young."

"I'm twenty-one," he said dully. "And I'm an old man."

"No, you're not. You've made one mistake. But it can be . . . rectified."

"How?"

Her nostrils flared a little and she looked at him defiantly. "Give yourself up."

That had never once occurred to Chapman. Not even in his most despondent moments. He stared stupidly at Evelyn. "But —they'll kill me. They'll hang—"

"No, they won't. Martin says if you pleaded guilty to the

bank robbery at Richfield, you'd be convicted of that alone."

"I don't believe it," Chapman said harshly. "They'd charge me with murder, too."

The light went out of Evelyn's eyes. "Then . . . you're going on?"

"I can't go back. Can't you see?" Desperately, he stared at her. "They killed Billy Bligh. They arrested my brother-in-law. They want me—and Clem Tancred. They wouldn't give us a chance. We fought on the wrong side in the war and they can't forgive us for that."

Evelyn turned partly away from Chapman. She said, "I'd hoped . . . you could find peace. I'm sorry for you, Jim Chapman."

He was sorry for himself. Sorry because of the thing he had seen in her eyes a few minutes ago. He could have reached out then and touched her . . . and he hadn't been able to do it. It was too late.

She turned at the door and said, "Good-bye . . . Jim."

He nodded dumbly and watched her go.

After Evelyn Comstock had gone, Chapman waited ten minutes. Then he left his room and paying his bill downstairs, went across the street to the Hoffman House. He found Clem and Dan Tancred in a smoke-filled room, playing cribbage.

They saw his sober face and Clem asked softly, "Well, Jim?"

"Halliday won't help Ed. The only thing that will—is ten thousand dollars."

Clem got up and reached for his coat. "There's ten thousand dollars in the Independence bank. Do we go for it?"

Chapman nodded.

In sight of Independence they put their horses into a canter and rode straight up the Kansas City road. It was excellent timing for the bank cashier was just in the act of unlocking the door of the bank. His teller, who had arrived earlier, was already waiting for his superior.

Clem Tancred and Chapman threw their reins to Dan and leaping to the ground, moved swiftly upon the bank officials. They did not draw their weapons until they were directly behind them, then each suddenly thrust a gun into a man's back.

"Inside," Chapman ordered viciously. "This is a holdup and we don't want any nonsense."

The frightened bank men stumbled into the room. Clem and Chapman shoved them along to the vault. "Open up this box and be damn quick about it!" Clem cried.

The cashier fumbled with a bunch of keys and dropped them finally. Chapman scooped them up and taking one at random stabbed it into the lock. It worked and he took off the lock and threw it to the floor.

Then he pulled out the inevitable wheat sack with which they had provided themselves. "Put all the money into that—all except the silver. I'll give you—thirty seconds!"

The cashier went into the vault. His trembling hands opened a steel box and he brought out stacks of money, which he thrust into the sack.

Chapman glanced back to look through the front window, to see that all was right with Dan Tancred outside.

"Jim!" cried Clem Tancred.

There were two explosions, one a gun in the palsied hand of the cashier inside the vault and the other Clem's. As Chapman whirled the cashier was crumpling to the floor. The teller bleated.

"Don't shoot me!"

Clem Tancred gave him a violent shove into the vault. "Then finish that job and hurry up, by damn!"

Jim Chapman was staring, fascinated at the cashier, lying upon the floor. The roof of the man's head had almost been blown off.

"I had to do it," Clem said.

Chapman nodded. Clem undoubtedly had saved his life; but they had taken a life, while engaged in a criminal enterprise. *There was no going back now.*

Outside the bank, Dan Tancred fired a warning shot. Immediately a half dozen guns roared. Chapman heard Dan Tancred's scream, "Come on, fellows! There's hell to pay!"

"That's enough," Chapman said, snatching the wheat sack from the teller's hands.

He turned and plunged for the door of the bank. Clem was at his side.

It was a glass door and as Chapman reached for it, the glass splintered into a thousand pieces. Chapman felt bee stings in two or three places.

They hit the sidewalk and Clem Tancred whistled. Up the street, a half dozen men with rifles and shotguns were advancing steadily upon the bank. Dan Tancred, in the saddle, was already bleeding from a gash on his forehead.

"Come on!" he cried frantically.

Chapman and Clem sprang for their horses, which Dan Tancred immediately released. They whirled them to gallop northward on the Freedom road and four horsemen were thundering down upon them from that direction.

That was something they could understand. A charge had to be met with a charge. Four to three odds was not too much. Clem Tancred let out a wild yell.

"Yip—yip—yee—oweee!"

Almost as if by a signal, the three bandits fired. One of the charging horses broke in its stride and plunged to the hard earth, throwing his rider. Another rider let out an awful scream and fell off his horse. The other two galloped past, on swerving horses.

Fourteen

DEEP IN THE ALMOST impenetrable brush that was east of Independence, the trio of bank robbers rested. This was country they knew from the old days. Federals had swarmed through it in companies and battalions and never had they routed the wartime guerrillas.

You could hear men thrashing in the underbrush a quarter of a mile away and you could merely slip aside and watch them pass; you could, if you were a guerrilla. A thousand men could not dislodge outlaws from this hilly jungle of shrub growth, not if the outlaws had friends near by to feed them and send warning whenever a determined man hunt was about to start.

They had the friends. Once he was in the brush, Chapman wondered why they had risked riding all the way to Iowa and dispersing the last time. This was where they should have come. Here into Nowhere.

They kept their horses saddled and hobbled, so they would not stray too far. There was plenty of forage for the animals and they would not suffer with the saddles on their backs during the day. At night they could be taken off.

They counted the loot. It totaled just short of $12,000.

Clem Tancred snorted when he learned the result. "That leaves us two thousand after we put up the ten thousand for Ed Taylor. Well, that's right, isn't it?"

"No," said Chapman, "I still have three thousand of my own. That goes into the pot. We share alike on everything. Money won't mean anything for a while, anyway. We've got to lay low. There's going to be a lot of activity around here. It may even get *too* hot. But before it does, I'm going to take this money to my sister."

"Now?" Clem asked.

"It's as good a time as any. They'll figure we're trying to put distance behind us. I'd better go alone, however."

He left the brothers and leading his horse, struck out in a northeasterly direction. It was seven or eight miles to his sister's home, and he shouldn't have any trouble getting there and started well on the return trip before darkness fell.

Now that the die was definitely cast, a load seemed lifted

from Chapman's mind. The thing he had been fearing most these last few weeks, he realized, was that having stepped overboard once, he would do it again. Now he had done it— and there was no going back.

He regretted the killing of the bank cashier, but it had been his life or the other man's. Clem had acted in the only manner possible. He would have done as much for Clem.

He recalled the first man he had ever killed; a fat German well in his forties—a Union militiaman. He had seen the man's face for days afterwards; until he had killed his second man.

That had been war. Well, so was this. They'd driven him into it—using the blue uniform of the old days. Retaliation was justified. If they called him an outlaw now instead of a guerrilla—what was the difference? His life was no more forfeit now than it had been during the war.

He crossed a narrow winding tote road and plunged into brush on the other side. After a while he hit the road running north of Freedom, within a half mile of where Pike and his ruffians had killed Welker and wounded Chapman a few weeks ago. A farmer was riding by on a mule and Chapman waited under cover until he had gone around a turn, before dashing across the open himself.

He was careful this time to approach the cabin from the side away from the Hobsons, remembering what Billy Bligh had said about his sister's neighbors being Yankee spies.

He made a half circle of the clearing and was disconcerted to see a man splitting wood behind the cabin. He waited for five minutes until the man stopped working and half-turning, wiped his face with a handkerchief. Then Chapman exclaimed in relief. It wasn't his brother-in-law, but it was Hutch Tompkins.

Hutch belonged to the right side. Tying his animal's reins to a sapling Chapman walked out into the clearing. Hutch saw him coming and recognized him instantly.

"Jim!" he cried. "You hadn't ought to come here."

Chapman shook hands with Hutch. "What're *you* doing here?"

"Well, Annie ain't fit for choppin' wood, so I figured mebbe I'd better come and help out a little. You know about Ed, don't you?"

"That's why I'm here. Where's Anne?"

Anne had already seen him from the back window. She came rushing around the side of the house. "Jim, come in the house—quick!"

He followed her. "Anyone been here today?"

"No, not today, but for weeks all sorts of men have been spying on us. They'd ride past in front and when we'd speak to them, they'd ask if this was the road to Centerville, or Freedom, or somewhere. And Ed'd see them in the woods."

"What you need," said Chapman bluntly, "is a good dog. One that'll sink his teeth into strangers."

"Ed got a dog. He was poisoned the third day we had him. But Jim . . ."

"Yes, Anne."

"You went and done it. Threw in with the Tancreds and the others. You did rob the Richfield bank, didn't you?"

Chapman looked thoughtfully at his sister. He said, "Look, Anne, the less you know about me, the better off you'll be. All I'll say is that Ed didn't have anything to do with that job. And I know that they threw him in jail to smoke me out. So . . . I brought you the money to put up for his bail."

He began pulling it out of his pockets. Anne stared.

"Then it's true!"

Chapman said deliberately, "Where's Tommy?"

She nodded to the bedroom. "Taking his afternoon nap. He—I suppose I have to take this money. We need Ed here now more than ever."

"Now?" Chapman asked sharply.

She nodded, flushing. "There's going to be another."

Chapman frowned. It was so true; the poor always had children. Ed could scrape but a bare living from his few acres of cleared land.

"All right," he said. "Get Ed out. They may not bring him to trial. But if they do, he'll be acquitted. They haven't got a thing against him. You'll get the bail money back, then. Keep it."

Hutch Tompkins came to the door and coughed loudly. When Chapman turned he gestured with his head.

Chapman went outside. "Dick Wood hallooed," Hutch told him. "He won't come up until I whistle. Is it all right?"

"Yes," said Chapman and after Hutch had put his fingers to his mouth and whistled twice, "Who started all this stuff?"

Hutch grinned. "Some of the boys. You know they're all with us—all the old-time Confederates, that is. Dick beat the hell out of a nosey Vickers man only two days ago."

"A Vickers man!" Chapman exclaimed. "How do you know he was a Vickers man? Did he admit it?"

"Uh-uh, he didn't admit anything. But what else would a

nosey stranger be around here. Hell, there been fifteen-twenty of them nosin' around since—well, since!"

Dick Wood suddenly materialized out of the woods. He stopped when he saw Jim Chapman, then broke into a run. "Jim!"

He shot a look at the house, then trotted to one side. Chapman and Hutch followed.

"I just got the news," Dick Wood said excitedly. "About Independence, I mean. Your sister know?"

Chapman shook his head. "Who told you?"

"It's all over Freedom. The minute I heard it I dashed over here."

"Why?"

Dick Wood reddened. "Aw, what the hell, Jim. You don't have to be that way with Hutch and me. Ain't Clem told you the fellas that was in on the Freedom thing?"

"I never asked him." Chapman looked at Hutch. "You, too?"

Hutch spread out his hands. "I bought me some good cows and a new plough and a seed drill."

"See?" Dick Wood said reproachfully. "And you should have told us before you went to Richfield. You got a nice haul, there."

"They lied. It was only fifteen thousand. How much do they say was taken at Independence?"

"Fifty thousand or more."

Chapman winced. "It was less than twelve. I just brought ten of it here to get Ed out of jail."

Dick Wood nodded. "Where's Clem?"

"In the brush. Dan's with him. That's all. You all know about Billy, of course."

Wood swore. "Gregg murdered him, the—! But Gregg's number is up. He knows it, too. Don't even dare ride out of Freedom any more. Somebody took a crack at him last week." Dick Wood smirked.

Hutch chuckled. "And that loud-mouthed George Pike, he took himself off on a trip to Minnesota or somewhere. I wonder if he'll be back."

Chapman looked narrowly at his friends. He sensed that things were changing around Freedom. "What about the soldiers?"

'Oh, they're still here. Only . . . they don't go out much at nights any more." Hutch put his tongue in his cheek. "It ain't going to be so healthy for the Vickers men any more—is it, Dick?"

Dick Wood smirked. "In a little while more you won't even have to hide in the brush, Jim."

Chapman shook his head. "It'll never be like that, fellows. The bank cashier at Independence was killed. . . ."

"Uh," said Dick, "and some dumb farmer, too. What of it?"

Chapman's eyes clouded. "They'll declare martial law."

"Nah, they won't," said Dick Wood. "Down in the southern part of the state, the folks have got together and they're riding around wearing white bed sheets and scarin' the hell out of the Yanks. Besides—don't you read the papers? There're some of our people in the legislature that was just elected. They can't do much yet, but they can squawk and in another year or two—well, Missouri always was a Democratic state. Except for the lop-eared Dutch."

Chapman thought a moment. "Dick, they know you beat up the detective?"

"No, I caught him alone. I don't think he even saw my face. Why, Jim?"

"Because we need someone who can go into town. If it's all right?"

"You know damn well it is. "

"And you, Hutch? You'll look over here until Ed gets out?"

"Count on that, Jim. When I can't make it Ed Sugrue comes here. Ed's all right, you know."

"Swell. I'd better go now. Dick . . . you can come along, if you want."

"All right, but my horse is over here. Where are you?"

Chapman pointed. He went back to the house, from where his sister was peering anxiously out of the door.

"Jim," she said, when he returned. "I don't like it. This money. . . . How did you get it?"

Chapman ignored the direct question. "Better go in to Freedom and get Ed to come home. Tell him I'll look in tomorrow night sometime."

"Will it be safe?"

He nodded. "It'll be all right. Just keep the light out."

There were six men in the band that robbed the Gallatin bank the day before Christmas. The new recruits were Dick Wood, Hutch Tompkins and Ed Sugrue. In February seven men rode into Centralia. Clark Welker had read the newspapers in Kentucky and returned to Missouri.

It was a week after the Centralia affair that Ed Taylor rode into the brush and handed Jim Chapman a letter. "It came in an envelope addressed to me. Here's the envelope."

Chapman stared at the soiled envelope. It was addressed, in ink, simply to Ed Taylor, Freedom, Missouri. But the postmark was Chicago, Illinois.

Ed had never been in Chicago in his life.

He looked at the second envelope. On it was written, "For Jim Chapman. Personal and Private. Please Forward."

Chapman put his thumb under the flap and ripped open the envelope. He took out the sheet of paper it contained and unfolded it.

His eyes widened. The letter written in a bold, scrawling hand, read:

DEAR JAMES BLAKE:

Our mutual friend—at whose home we visited during your recent sojourn in this city—has asked me to write this letter to you. He thinks it will bear more weight coming from me.

Our friend has expressed several times his disappointment in your sudden departure from Chicago and believes it would have been to your advantage to talk things over with him. He is still of that opinion and wonders if you could not come and see him in Chicago—or if that is inconvenient, to arrange a suitable meeting place.

I am empowered to assure you that this meeting will be in the strictest confidence and nothing will be done to jeopardize your position.

The undersigned gives his personal pledge in addition to our friend's and wishes to say that wheat is still going down. Awaiting your reply with the deepest interest, and sympathy, I beg to remain,

Your Obedient Servant

PHILIP CASTLEMON

Chapman read the letter twice, then slowly folded it and put it away in his pocket.

"Bad news, Jim?"

Chapman's mouth twisted. "No. It's from a friend; a friend I didn't know I had."

Later, he spread the letter face down on his saddle and with a stub of pencil started to write a reply. Finally, however, he tore the sheet of paper in half and applied a match to both halves.

Clem Tancred, stretched out on a blanket near by, said, "Love letter, Jim?" He grinned to soften the jibe.

Chapman winced. The shot came too close to his thoughts.

It was because of Evelyn Comstock that he had started to write a reply to Philip Castlemon's letter.

He hadn't seen her since Kansas City. She had given him his chance there and he had rebuffed her. He had made his decision and that was the end of it.

That was more than four months now. Yet, during those four months he had contrived, every week, to obtain a copy of the Freedom *Herald,* ostensibly to keep up with the activities of The Other Side, but actually, to read the social news of Freedom. He saw her name—often. But there was never any mention of the approaching nuptials. Halliday's name was still linked with hers, however. The paper said: "Miss Evelyn Comstock attended the Methodist Church Supper in company with Mr. Martin Halliday, our rising young attorney."

Chapman said to Clem Tancred, "I may take a little trip to Chicago."

Clem sat up. "I'll go with you. I'm getting tired of this loafing around. I want to get some books."

"Books, Clem?"

Clem flushed. "You know I always read a lot. I like history —ancient history. I saw an advertisement in the Kansas City *Star* about a new set on the old Roman stuff. I'd like to get it."

Fifteen

CHAPMAN SAID to the doorman of the Board of Trade, "I'd appreciate it if you'd take a mesage to Mr. Philip Castlemon, the trader, and inform him that his friend, Mr. Blake of Missouri, would like to see him." He pushed a greenback into the uniformed man's hand.

One minute later, Philip Castlemon, leaner than ever, came striding up to the door. "Blake!" he exclaimed with pleasure, "I'm glad you came." His handclasp was sincere.

Chapman didn't know until then how much he had missed his brief friendship with the Chicago wheat trader. That day with him, months ago, had been one of the most enjoyable of his life. He had been content.

"I'm sorry I ran out that night, Castlemon."

"It's all right. Shall we go to Al's office? He's in the city, even though we weren't expecting to see you quite so soon."

Chapman hesitated. "Do you mind? I've a friend with me and for his sake—I'd rather the meeting was not prearranged."

Castlemon reddened. "I understand," he said, a bit stiffly. "You must be cautious. Well—how do you want to arrange it?"

"Send a messenger to his office. Have Mr. Vickers come to the Palmer House alone. You meet him there and take a carriage. Drive west on Madison Street and somewhere along the road I will meet you."

Castlemon bowed. "In about a half hour?"

"Yes."

They parted and Chapman frowned as he watched the wheat trader walk stiffly across the street to a telegraph office. Castlemon was a gentleman, he wasn't used to having his word doubted—but too much water had flowed under the Chicago bridge since the autumn before.

On Adams Street he rented a rig and putting the whip to the horse drove it swiftly up Madison Street for a mile and a half. He allowed the horse to rest for a few minutes then, before beginning a more leisurely drive eastward.

On the bridge crossing the river he stopped to watch a flatboat drift by underneath. When he shook out the lines, he

saw Vickers and Castlemon in a carriage coming toward him.
The block was almost deserted and there were only one or two
carriages in sight, none close.

Chapman pulled over to meet them, made a wide turn and
came up from the rear. He called, "Would you mind exchang-
ing places with me, Mr. Castlemon?"

"Of course not."

Vickers stopped his carriage and Castlemon climbed down
and came over to Chapman's carriage. Chapman got out and
walked forward.

Alan Vickers' face was grim. He did not offer to shake
hands and Chapman climbed in stiffly. Vickers touched the
horse's flank with the edge of his whip and the animal trotted
away.

"You should have accepted that job last summer," Vickers
said, by way of beginning.

"I told you then I was a Confederate."

"You didn't tell me you'd been a guerrilla. But I'd have
overlooked even that. Now—I don't mind telling you, Chapman, you're in pretty deep. However, I've a proposition to
make you. Surrender and stand trial for the Richfield job—
and we won't press any of the others."

"We?" Chapman asked bluntly.

"Of course. The banks have to continue business in Confederate territory. The railroads are my clients. Do you know
that their business has fallen off ten per cent since you began
operations in Missouri?"

Chapman exclaimed. "How could anything that I've done
affect the railroads?"

"You've scared people out of Missouri," Vickers said
grimly. "The newspapers all over the country have played up
these things. They're calling Missouri the Outlaw State. People
aren't going to settle there. Mercantile firms are asking for
cash from Missouri businessmen. They say they can't extend
credit there, because the banks are not safe. The Cagel bank
in Freedom closed its doors. So did the Richfield bank. . . ."

"The Cagel bank was reopened by Major Comstock,"
Chapman retorted. "Less than fifteen thousand was lost in the
Richfield bank. . . ."

Vickers' eyes glittered. "They claimed forty thousand. I
wonder—well, never mind. As I said, the railroads want the
Missouri gang broken up. They're more interested in that
than they are in sending the bandits to the penitentiary for
long terms. They're willing to go easy on you fellows. . . ."

"Fellows?"

"Of course. There are a half dozen of you, at least."

Chapman stiffened. "Are you asking that I surrender them?"

Vickers turned sidewards. "I am asking that. They'll get off with light sentences. Probably not more than five or ten years."

"And I?"

Vickers moistened his lips with his tongue. "Ten. Fifteen at the outside. I promise you that."

A slow flush began at the base of Chapman's throat and worked up into his face. This was a new Alan Vickers. He was showing claws that had been sheathed before .

Chapman said curtly, "I'm sorry, Mr. Vickers. I can't speak for the others. I wouldn't, if I could. As for myself—"

"Wait!" Vickers cut in sharply. "Before you answer I want you to know the alternative."

"Yes?"

Vickers cleared his throat bruskly. "The alternative . . . is extinction. I mean that, Chapman. Up to now, we've stepped around gently. Pussyfooted, because we haven't wanted to tread on the gentle Confederate toes. I've been out there in your country. I know that everyone's secretly for you. They aid and abet you—because they think you're fighting Yanks. They're wrong and you know it. That's why I'm telling you now what's going to happen—"

"Will you stop the carriage?" Chapman said coldly.

Vickers gripped Chapman's arm in a hand of steel. "Hear me through. I've got the biggest detective organization in this country. I've got offices in twenty-two cities. Two hundred men work for me full time and I can hire five hundred more any time I want. Even today people don't know what our organization did during the war. Did *you* know we had three men inside Pemberton's lines at Vicksburg? Did you know there were Vickers men with Lee in Virginia? Why, I even had a man on the staff of Joe Johnston!

"I've got good men, Chapman. I haven't used them, so far. But I'm going to now. The railroads are desperate and they insist on results. I'll go so far as to tell you that they've given me an ultimatum. And loss of their contracts would just about ruin me financially. This is a life and death matter with me, too. Chapman, you come in or by God, I'll turn my entire organization loose on you. Every man who carries a Vickers badge."

"I'll think it over," Chapman said brefly.

Vickers' mouth opened and closed for a moment like that of a fish out of water. "You won't believe me!"

"Oh, yes, I do believe you. I don't think I ever under-estimated you, Mr. Vickers. It's just that—I want to think it over. . . ."

Vickers shook his head in despair. "Then, I've got to play my last card. My ace in the hole. I'd hoped I wouldn't have to do it."

He sawed on the reins and made a complete U-turn in West Madison Street. Chapman's hand came swiftly across and touched the lapel of his sackcloth coat. "Where are you going?" he demanded.

"Downtown. Oh, it's all right. I gave my word. You're in no danger. I just want you to see someone."

"No," Chapman said. "You can let me out here."

"This person," said Vickers deliberately, "is someone you know. I brought her here for this purpose. Her name is . . . Evelyn Comstock."

For a moment Chapman held his breath. Then he let it out slowly. "What do you know about Evelyn Comstock?"

"I told you my organization is a big one." Vickers laughed shortly. "I saw the letter you wrote to Martin Halliday before he saw it, Chapman. I could have come to Kansas City then and taken you. I didn't want to. . . . I made a small mistake. I thought when she went to you that she could win you over. . . ."

They passed Philip Castlemon still driving westward. Chapman stared at the flimsy false-fronted stores along Madison. He said, "What else do you know?"

"I know that you and all your men have spent the entire winter in Clay County, that you've been going openly from place to place, that you've slept in the brush very few nights. Oh, don't worry about that. There are no traitors among your friends. I'm just trying to tell you that I know what's going on. And as for Miss Comstock . . . she is a remarkable girl. She would marry you—yes, even now, if you gave it up."

"What good would that do?" Chapman asked dully. "If I went to prison for fifteen years."

"You're twenty-one," Vickers said crisply. "You're still a boy. In ten years—and it wouldn't be more than that—you'd still be young. She would wait. . . ."

Yes, he was only twenty-one. But five of those years had been lived during a war. A year of such war was ten years in ordinary life. Chapman was old—as old as Alan Vickers.

"Where is she?" he asked suddenly.

"At the Palmer House. I sent a message over the moment I got Castlemon's. She's waiting."

She was sitting on a mohair sofa when they entered her room. She got up when she saw Chapman. Her mouth was open and there was a frightened look in her eyes.

"Evelyn," he said thickly.

Her eyes went to Vickers. The detective shook his head. "It's up to you, Miss Comstock."

Chapman said, "Mr. Vickers thinks I should surrender. He assures me that I can get off with ten or fifteen years."

Pain and shock twisted her face. "Oh, no!" she cried. "You couldn't. It would—it would kill you."

Alan Vickers exclaimed in surprise, tinged with anger, "It won't hurt him. Ten years isn't much. He's young."

"But you don't understand," Evelyn protested. "Someone else—perhaps not. But Jim—Jim would die locked up. You—you didn't tell me this. . . ."

Chapman stared at her, fascinated. He had actually known her so few minutes. How had she come to understand him? How could she know that that was true what she said; that he would never survive ten years in a prison? He looked at her and the hot blood throbbed in his temples.

Alan Vickers groaned. "It's going to be war, then, Chapman?"

Chapman did not reply. He said to Evelyn Comstock, "Thanks."

A smile quavered on her lips. Suddenly Alan Vickers was not with them, the room in fact, disappeared. They were alone —as alone as if they had met in the Missouri brush. Chapman took a step forward and then she was in his arms, sobbing and trembling.

For a long moment they stood like that and then Vickers' voice came to them, as if from a great distance.

"Good-bye, Chapman. You have twenty-four hours."

Chapman heard the door open and close and then he released Evelyn. "It's going to be hell," he said softly. "You'll never have a home. And someday—someday they'll—"

Her hand touched his lips to stop the words. "I don't care. I'll go with you . . . anywhere."

They were married an hour later. Clem Tancred, big, bewildered Clem, went with them to the minister's residence on West Adams Street. He followed them to the train, where Chapman placed Evelyn in a seat by the window. Clem went outside then and waited, ten minutes, until the train began moving and Chapman dropped off.

He looked at Chapman's tight face and sighed heavily. "Now what, Jim?"

Chapman shook his head. Tersely he told Clem of his talk with Alan Vickers, the latter's ultimatum. Clem gasped, when Chapman finished.

"And you married her just the same?"

"I married her," Chapman said savagely. "They may get me, but I'll have that. I've never had anything in my life before, but I have now. I'm going to strike the first blow, too—a blow they'll never forget. Maybe they'll come to my terms, then."

Clem stared .

"It isn't the banks," Chapman went on. "Vickers is working for the railroads. They're the ones that are after us. All right, we'll give the railroads something to think about."

"What are you going to do, Jim? You can't—"

"I can. Send a telegram to your cousin in Harrisonville. . . . I don't trust them at Freedom. Have him ride to the boys at once and tell them to meet us in Omaha. We're going to stop the Union Pacific train!"

Sixteen

THE AGENT in the red-painted little station on which the name *Cedar Hill* had been stenciled in white letters, leaned back in his armchair and put his feet upon the table containing his telegraph instruments. Outside the wicket, three or four local farmers talked idly about the condition of the winter wheat and the possibilities of a good corn crop.

The agent was waiting for the eastbound passenger train to clear through Cedar Hill, after which he could lock up the depot and go home. Another ten minutes.

He yawned.

The door of the waiting room opened and three men entered. One of them came directly to the wicket opening into the agent's cubicle.

The agent turned his head curiously—and his chair crashed over backwards.

"Get up—with your hands in the air!" curtly ordered the man at the window. The huge Navy Colt in his fist reflected the light from the hanging lamp above.

In the waiting room, the farmers were standing, ashen-faced, with their hands raised. Two more men came into the station. Like the previous ones, they wore linen dusters and carried revolvers.

One of them pushed in the door of the agent's room and roughly shoved the agent to one side. He brought a pair of wire cutters from the pocket of his duster and began cutting wires on the telegraph instrument. He wound up by throwing the key to the floor and jumping on it.

Finished with that task, he said to the agent, "Get out now and set your signals to stop the train."

"But I can't," the agent chattered. "It only stops here when there are passengers. The rules—"

The bandit thrust his revolver under the agent's nose. "Here are your rules!"

Chapman was standing alone on the platform when Ed Sugrue came out with the agent. He nodded.

The agent set his signals, then, under Sugrue's direction, got three or four lanterns and lit them. He lined them up on the platform.

Chapman said: "Lock them up inside now. The whole bunch of them. Then you'd better climb up the pole there and cut the wires. Just to be safe."

Dick Wood had caught the horse job today and was back in the thicket a hundred yards. The other six outlaws posted themselves on both sides of the tracks. They held lanterns under their dusters, so the lights would not show too soon to the train crew.

They were ready when the long beam of the searchlight cut the darkness about them.

The engine whistle blasted twice and the wheels of the train began grinding on sand. The engine came to a stop, directly opposite the station. Chapman swung up on the fire platform from the left side. At the same moment, Clem Tancred's broad face appeared opposite.

"This is a holdup," Chapman said grimly to the fireman and engineer.

The engineer blinked in astonishment. "Holdup? . . . Wh-what for?"

"For what's in the express car," snapped Clem Tancred. "Come on, climb down to the ground."

The trainmen obeyed and the outlaws followed. Dan Tancred and Hutch Tompkins were already pounding on the door of the express car.

"Open up in there!" cried Hutch.

Down by the passenger coaches, men began jumping to the ground. The conductor, a small revolver in his hand, was running toward the bandits, shouting, "Here, here, what's going on here?"

Ed Sugrue laughed and fired his revolver over the conductor's head. That gentleman immediately dropped his little pistol.

Chapman called to the conductor. "Come here, you. Tell the express messenger to open up his door, or we'll put dynamite under the car."

His knees knocking together, the conductor approached. "Quincy!" he called. "You'd better open up. They—they're armed."

A rifle bullet tore through the door of the express car.

"All right, boys," said Chapman. "Put the dynamite under the car."

They had no dynamite but for a moment or two Hutch and Dan scrambled around under the car. They bumped a wheel, tapped on the bottom of the car, and then the express messenger called from inside, "If you won't kill me, I'll open up."

"Open up," replied Chapman. "We haven't killed anyone yet. Throw your rifle out first, though. . . ."

The door was slid open a few inches and a Winchester thrown out. Then the messenger opened the door wide. Chapman gestured him down to the ground, then he and Clem Tancred climbed into the car with their lanterns.

Clem headed for the registered mail pouches. "The hell with them," Chapman said. "What we want'll be in the safe. Call that messenger in here."

When the messenger climbed back into the car, white-faced, Chapman said to him, "Now, Quincy, you're a loyal employee of the express company. They pay you a good salary—but no salary is enough for you to give your life for the railroad. Is it?"

"N-no, sir," replied the messenger.

"Good, then find your key and open up that safe."

Terror split the messenger's face. "I—I c-can't, sir. That's a through safe. They've got the key for it in Chicago."

Clem Tancred thrust a Navy at the man's head. "Open it before I count three."

The messenger fell to his knees and Chapman waved Tancred back. "I think he's telling the truth. Well, next time we'll have to bring that dynamite after all. See if you can't find something to break the thing open."

Clem began tearing up the express car. After a couple of minutes' search, he came up with an axe. He smashed it against the door of the safe and the axe ricocheted off the iron door and sunk itself into the wooden wall of the car.

Clem cursed and began yanking at the handle. His big shoulder brushed a pile of boxes beside the safe and the top box fell down and barked Clem's shin. He yelped in pain and kicked the offending box viciously.

It bounced to Chapman's feet. He started to brush it aside, then exclaimed, "Hold on, Clem!"

He stooped and hit the thin boards of the box, already split, with the barrel of his Navy Colt. The board splintered and Chapman reached in and pulled out a sheaf of green paper.

"I think this is what we want, Clem," he said, in a strained voice.

"Yow!" Clem cried. He turned and grabbed another of the boxes. Instantly he swore. "No, this is too heavy." He hurled the box to the floor. It broke open and a shower of gold coins spilled over the floor.

"Gawd!" he cried.

Chapman walked to the door of the train. "Dan—Hutch, come in here. We need some help."

There was only the one box of paper currency, but there were four of gold coin and another of silver. Chapman estimated the value of the silver box and decided against it. Too heavy for what it was worth.

They broke the boxes open and dumped the contents into two wheat sacks. They were so heavy a man could scarcely carry one.

Outside, Chapman fired twice into the air to apprise Dick Wood of the completion of their task. The whole thing had occupied fifteen minutes.

Chapman said to the engineer, "Get into your cab, now and pull it up two miles. We're going to go through the passenger cars and if you come back inside of a half hour, some of the passengers are going to get hurt."

The fireman uncoupled the engine from the rest of the train and the engineer climbed into his cab and started off with the engine. The moment the engine was out of sight around a bend, Chapman turned to his men. "All right, boys, let's beat it. This'll give us a little start."

A hundred yards away they found Dick Wood with the horses and almost a nervous wreck from the suspense. "It go all right?" he cried.

Then he saw the heavy wheat sacks and whistled.

Ten miles from the scene of the Cedar Hill train robbery the seven outlaws spread a blanket on the ground and counted the proceeds. It was a stunning amount.

One hundred and two thousand dollars!

Soberly, Chapman divided the money. "There's going to be hell about this—even in Clay County. I don't think any of us ought to go there—for a long while. You know the code; keep in touch that way, but be careful. We oughtn't to get together for six months at least. During that time . . . be careful, fellows."

Seventeen

TWO DAYS LATER, Chapman, wearing a swallow tail coat and a tight-fitting derby hat, got off the train at the little German village of Waverly, in north-central Iowa. He had reached the town by a roundabout route, from western Iowa cutting straight across the state and embarking on a northbound steamboat. At Dubuque he had got off and changed to a west-bound train.

According to Chapman's reasoning no one would look for a former Confederate soldier in a German Republican strong-hold. But when he looked down the amazingly broad street, lined with trees, and saw the freshly painted stores and houses, a strange feeling of peace came over him.

This town was new and clean. As he walked down the street he could almost believe that the wooden sidewalks had been scrubbed that day.

There was a two-story frame hotel a block from the river. It had a sign outside, *Vogel's Hotel, Rooms and Board.* Chapman went into the clean little lobby and a stout, middle-aged woman got up from a rocking chair in which she had been knitting.

"Guten Morgen," she said.

"Good morning," Chapman replied. "I wonder if I could get a room for a week or two. A large room, for my wife will be coming from Chicago in about a week."

"Ja, sure. Natürlich," said Mrs. Vogel. "Berhaps you would like two rooms, togedder. Mit meals, I can give dem for you for ten dollars."

"That would be splendid. My name is John Simmons. I am thinking of buying a farm around here."

"A farm?" exclaimed Mrs. Vogel. "Ach, you have gome to the right place. Farms is so goot here. Rich—what you call —eart'. You talk to Mr. Vogel, when he gome home at noon. But now I show you your rooms."

Chapman walked about the village later. At the railroad station he saw a bundle of newspapers thrown from a train and followed the bundle on the shoulders of a stalwart youth to a tobacco store up the street.

He bought a pouch of tobacco and on his way out pre-

93

tended to notice the newspapers and bought one. He rolled it up casually and stuck it under his arm. He strolled about town a few minutes more, then went to his rooms at the Vogel Hotel.

Eagerly he spread out the paper and winced when he saw the headlines:

Railroad Offers $25,000 Reward for Jim Chapman. Most Spectacular Robbery in History. Quarter Million Dollar Bandits Sought in Missouri. Alan Vickers Declares He Will Make Arrest Soon

Chapman started to read the details of the story, but a phrase in italics leaped from the page. *Dead or Alive,* it read. He read the account and a fine film of perspiration came to his face. Vickers was out to fulfill his ultimatum issued in Chicago. A telegraphic dispatch from Kansas City, printed on page 2, told of a hundred detectives, armed with shotguns, rifles and revolvers, invading Clay County from the west. They were determined, the dispatch said, to get the bandits and quell outlawry in the Outlaw State, once and for all. The detectives were being reinforced by a company of soldiers under the command of Major Peterson, the provost marshal at Freedom.

Finished reading, Chapman stared at the paper for a long time. There was no mention in it, anywhere, of Evelyn Comstock. Surely, Vickers knew. He must have followed Chapman's trail in Chicago. Why then was he withholding that information? Had he learned that Evelyn had not gone to St. Louis? That she got off the train at Springfield and from there went to Indianapolis?

Were Vickers men following her even now?

Would she bring them to Waverly, Iowa, on her roundabout trip to this rendezvous?

He was still thinking about it when Mrs. Vogel tapped on his door and announced that lunch was ready downstairs. At the table were a half-dozen townsfolk. Also Mr. Vogel, a fat German with amazingly long mustaches.

"My vife tells me you are looking for a good farm, Mr. Simmons," he said to Chapman. "My brother-in-law has farm he would like sell. He is getting old and vould like to moof to the city. Is very fine farm. You like to see?"

"Why, yes," said Chapman. "I'd like very much to see it." And all the while he was thinking, what's the use? I'll only have to move again.

Yet, when Mr. Vogel came around to the hotel with a rig he climbed in beside the German and rode with him two miles east of the town. There, Vogel turned in toward a whitewashed stone house, a house with a broad veranda. Near by were whitewashed barns and outbuildings and an orchard of apple trees.

Chapman looked at the farm and compared it mentally with the scrubby Clay County land. He shook his head when a man who could have been an older brother of Martin Vogel instead of a brother-in-law came out of the house and wiped his hands on his clean overalls.

"Mr. Simmons," said Vogel, "this is Johann Mueller. Johann, Mr. Simmons vants to buy a farm."

The farmer's eyes lit up. "Ja! Then you buy this one. It is eighty acres and almost half of it cleared land. The voods is fine for pasture. I have three goot horses, one of dem for the buggy. There is two cows and eighteen pigs. Chickens and twelve goose. I sell everyt'ing, mit the machinery and all—seven t'ousand dollars. You pay me one t'ousand dollar cash and the bank gif the mor'gage for the odder?"

"Why," said Chapman. "My uncle in Ireland left me a little money, but I won't get it for a few more weeks. However, I can pay three thousand dollars now."

As quickly as that Chapman bought a farm. They drove into Waverly and the papers were signed and Chapman paid Johann Mueller three thousand dollars.

When they left the bank, Mueller said: "I am mofing Saturday. Already, I have rented house in Waverly."

The next morning, Chapman received a letter. It said merely, "Dear Husband: I will arrive Sunday morning by train. Love, Your wife."

Chapman went out to the farm on Thursday. Mr. and Mrs. Mueller showed him around the place and then summoned a man from a neighboring farm, a rough, uncouth youth named Hans Schnabel. Chapman hired him. He looked sincere enough.

He remained on the farm and saw the Muellers off in the farm wagon on Saturday. It was piled high with their personal possessions, although they had sold the meager furniture along with the house and farm.

Chapman slept in the farmhouse alone that night. It was long before he went to sleep, however. He did not know what the morrow would bring. Evelyn, yes, but—what else?

He was a married man, now. Married a week and he had placed his bride on the train an hour after the ceremony. He

had known her perhaps a half hour altogether in the months
since he had first met her.

As a child she had gone through the chaos that was Order
Number 11, but she had lived a sheltered life of recent years.
How would she react to the sort of life Chapman could give
her?

In the morning, he got Hans to harness the "buggy" horse
to the rig and drove to Waverly. He was at the depot a half
hour before the train came in, yet when it finally chugged
to a stop, he stepped away to one side.

His eyes darted along the cars. An elderly couple got off;
a woman with a child, then a man in overalls and . . . a
heavy-set man in a business suit. Chapman's eyes remained
on the last man, so that Evelyn had stepped down from the
steps and was standing on the platform looking about for
him, before he caught sight of her.

He took a deep breath then, and walked toward her. She
gave a glad cry when she saw him and came instantly into
his arms. He kissed her, but his eye was still on the heavy-set
man. He gathered up her bags and boxes that the porter set
down on the platform, gave the man a dollar and with a
glance over his shoulder hurried to the rig beside the depot.

Scarcely had he helped her in and climbed in himself than
he said, "That heavy-set man who got out before you? . . ."

She exclaimed, softly, "What man? I didn't notice?"

"Turn around," he said grimly. "The man in the brown-
black broadcloth suit."

Wonderingly, she obeyed, then said, "Why—he's a minister. He got on the train at Oelwein. I heard him talking to
the conductor. They—they don't all wear the turned collar."

Relief flooded through Chapman. Relief so great that he
actually became garrulous. "I bought a farm, Evelyn. It's the
cleanest, neatest farm you ever saw. Not at all like the
Missouri farms. . . ."

"I'll love it, Jim," Evelyn said quietly. "I told you in Chicago I'd go wherever you went . . . only . . . don't leave
me again. I don't think I could stand it."

Looking straight ahead, he asked, "You've read about Cedar Hill? . . ."

She bowed her head slightly. "Jim . . . I'd rather not talk
about that . . ."

He laughed suddenly. "Look at this town. Did you ever see
one laid out like this—with such ridiculously wide streets?
And look at those trees on each side. But wait—wait until
you see the farm. You've never seen anything . . ."

She responded instantly to his cheerfulness and before they had cleared the village her hand was on his arm and she was laughing.

When he turned in to the whitewashed buildings, however, she fell silent. He leaped to the ground and lifted her down, and then she whispered, "It's wonderful, Jim!"

Eighteen

JIM CHAPMAN lived on the Iowa farm one month. During that brief interlude he knew the sweat of honest toil. He ploughed and he planted. He worked all day in the fields and he was tired and laughed when he went to the cool, whitewashed house at noon and in the evening.

Evelyn kept the house as scrubbed as had her German predecessor. She sang while she worked and a glow came to her cheeks.

Chapman almost forgot.

Then one day a heavy-set man climbed down from a rig and walked across the field to where Chapman was working. His face beamed with good fellowship and he held out a meaty hand.

"How are you, my friend? It's a grand day to be out in the country, isn't it? My name is Billings and I represent the American Harvester Company."

"How do you do, Mr. Billings."

"Fine. Fine. How long have you been farming here, Mr. Simmons? It's a grand farm, but you'll be needing a thresh-ing machine with all this wheat you're growing."

The green blades were two inches tall. But they were oats, not wheat. Chapman felt a little cold, even though the sun was high in the sky.

He said, "Why, I couldn't afford to buy a threshing ma-chine. The Bachman Brothers have a machine and they usu-ally travel from farm to farm, you know. . . ."

"Of course, of course! No harm trying though, is there? But now, we have a disking machine, a brand-new model that's just about the finest thing you ever saw."

Billings went on. He talked about cultivators, seed drills. He touched on the war and asked Chapman questions about his personal history. But he never brought out catalogs of his machinery and never quoted an actual price.

The next day a man wearing overalls applied for work. He was a big, strapping fellow and so eager for a good place that he offered to work for one half of what Chapman paid Hans Schnabel, his hired man.

Two days later came the men from the farm paper. Two of them. They were both big men.

"You've certainly got a fine farm here, Mr. Simmons," one of them said. "You're no doubt interested in keeping up with all the latest farm news. The *Iowa Farm Reporter* covers this state like a blanket. It prints all the latest news and information on farming and it costs you only a dollar a year."

"All right." said Chapman, "put me down for a year."

"Thank you, sir. You spell your name with two 'M's', don't you, Mr. Simmons? Uh, have you ever taken our paper before, Mr. Simmons? No? Oh, you're from out of state— Wisconsin? Missouri? A grand state. . . ."

When the men had gone, Chapman turned his team of horses over to Hans. He walked to the whitewashed house and entered the kitchen from the rear.

Evelyn was taking a cake from the big oven. He watched her a moment, his eyes bleak, then he said, "It's come, Evelyn."

Startled, she set the cake pan on the top of the stove. He saw the fear in her eyes and his throat constricted so that he could scarcely whisper.

"We've got to go."

"You mean—leave the farm?"

Then without waiting for an answer she went to the bedroom. She came out immediately with a bag already packed. "I kept it packed," she said bravely.

He shook his head. "You'll have to buy new things. I think it would be better if we just drove off in the rig, without any luggage. We'll drive through Waverly, to Shell Rock."

Evelyn took the bag to the bedroom. She returned, wearing an everyday sunbonnet. She went out with him, while he harnessed a horse to the rig.

Then they drove leisurely, through Waverly, to Shell Rock, six miles away. They left the horse outside a store while they made a few minor purchases.

They sauntered to the railroad station, just as the train came in. There was no time to purchase tickets, so they bought them on the train. It was a northbound train. Chapman, who was familiar with railroad timetables, knew that St. Paul was the end of the line. He paid for their passage to St. Paul.

When the train stopped at Albert Lea, early in the evening, Chapman and Evelyn got off. They bought some candy in the station, then went through and walked into the town. He rented a rig at the livery stable and they drove through the night, to Winona.

In the morning they boarded a southbound train for Madison, Wisconsin. There they stayed at a hotel for a couple of days, then rented a cottage on Monona Lake.

They lived in the cottage for almost a month, but it was not the same as the farm in Iowa. They remained indoors most of the day, going down to the lake only in the evenings. Chapman went to Madison every few days, making purchases of food . . . and newspapers.

There were other cottages along the lake and as the season progressed, they began to fill.

Leaving their lamps burning, Chapman and Evelyn went to Madison one evening and boarded the stagecoach for Peoria, Illinois. There they took the train to Clinton, where they transferred to the river steamer for St. Louis.

They remained overnight in St. Louis, at the Planters Hotel, where Chapman registered himself and Evelyn as Captain Lucius Parker and Wife, of Memphis, Tennessee.

The next day he bought a new Prince Albert of gray broadcloth material. Evelyn did some shopping for herself and in the evening they walked across the gangplank of the *City of Chattanooga*.

Chapman gambled in the saloon and talked of trying tobacco instead of cotton. He drank more than was his custom and thought that he gave the impression of being a Southern cotton planter, who had not become too impoverished by the war.

Yet, their hotel room was searched the first day they stayed in Nashville. They went to Louisville and then to Pittsburgh. They stayed there a week and nothing happened. It looked as if they had lost them, so to make sure, they went on to New York.

They rented the ground floor of a brownstone house on West Sixteenth Street and furnished it with secondhand furniture that Chapman thought was in keeping with the house and neighborhood.

The tautness left Evelyn's face and the sparkle came again to her eyes. She made friends with Mrs. Kielty who lived over them on the second floor. Mrs. Kielty gave Evelyn some homemade jelly and brought her a half of a cake one day.

She said. "It's a shame that your husband hasn't been able to find a job in all these weeks. That's the trouble with this country, too many foreigners coming in and a good American citizen can't get himself an honest job of work."

When Evelyn told him about it, Chapman shook his head. "I've got to get a job."

He got one the day following—as a stevedore on the docks. It was backbreaking work, but Chapman didn't mind. He hadn't minded the hard work on his farm in Iowa.

He came home from work at seven o'clock every evening and after supper he and Evelyn went for walks. On Saturday evenings they went to the theater and on Sundays they often hired a rig and went for a drive.

Then one day a fat man came down to the docks. He smoked a fat, black cigar and had a pocketful of greenbacks. He talked to the dockwallopers and handed out dollar bills, one to every man. Two husky assistants passed around a bottle and cigars, the latter not quite as fat or black as the fat man was smoking.

He came up to Chapman. "Sure and you're votin' the good, old Republican ticket," he said. "Here's a dollar for the trouble you'll be havin' and here's a good ten-cent cigar. Furthermore, it's open house at Paddy's Saloon all day and it's General Grant we want in the White House to teach them goddam Confederates that they was nothin' but black traitors and as such they should be treated."

Chapman took the dollar and the cigar. He tore the dollar in half and threw it into the fat man's face. The cigar he ground under his foot.

"I don't take pay for voting," he said.

"A black Confederate!" the fat man yelped. "A traitor to his country and takin' the bread out of the mouths of honest patriots, who fought for their country. Timothy! Mike! . . ."

The two thugs put down their bottles and boxes of cigars and leaped upon Chapman. Chapman side-stepped their first rush and struck one of the men on the side of his head, knocking him off the dock into the dirty water below.

Then he whirled upon the second man and drove him to his knees with a salvo of savage blows. The fat politician danced around Chapman.

"Help, murder, police! Confed'rate soldiers!"

Chapman was slapping the fat man's mouth when the helmeted police came. They took him to the precinct house and there the fat politician took the sergeant into a private room. When the latter came out a few minutes later he looked blackly at Chapman.

"So it's a Confederate you are, me lad? New York ain't the place for the likes of you. . . ."

"This man tried to bribe me to vote for Grant," Chapman said coldly. "Even if I *was* a Republican I wouldn't take a bribe."

"So it's a lawyer, you want? All right, if that's your wish, ye can have one. But it may take a while. Say, until tomorrow when the returns are in and General Grant has become President."

Chapman spent the night in the cell. The next day he paced the cubicle until late in the afternoon, when they released him. He walked as swiftly as he could to West Sixteenth Street.

When she saw him, Evelyn fainted.

Later, revived, she said to him, "It was a mistake, Jim. I thought I could go through with it, but I can't. I can't bear to see you step out of the house, for fear you'll never come back. I can't sleep at night because I hear sounds in the house. I can't walk down the street without thinking someone is following. . . . Jim, I want to go home."

"All right, Evelyn," Chapman said. "Go home. I'll take a trip to Europe. In a year or two, perhaps. . . ."

"Yes, Jim! Perhaps, it'll blow over. . . ."

Perhaps.

He took Evelyn to the train and then, with only a carpetbag for baggage, went to the East River Pier, where there was a boat sailing for Cuba.

As he approached the gangplank a big man stepped up to him. "Your name Simmons, Mister?"

"Sorry," said Chapman, "it's Steadman."

"Maybe so, but you answer the description of a man who was arrested at the docks for attacking a precinct worker. I think you'd better come along and have a talk with the chief at the office."

"No," said Chapman, "my boat sails in a few minutes. I've arranged for passage."

The big man took out the passenger list. "And you say your name's Steadman? There's no Steadman on here . . . ."

Chapman smashed the man in the face. Then he dropped his carpetbag and ran from the pier.

Alan Vickers sat in his big office on Michigan Avenue, in Chicago. He picked up a sheet of yellow paper from his desk and read it for the tenth or eleventh time. Finally he got up and went to the door. He opened it and crooked a finger at a lean young man in his early twenties.

"Fenton, come into my office."

When Fenton entered, Vickers handed him the yellow sheet of paper, which was a telegram.

Fenton looked at it and read:

Chapman's wife on Chicago-bound train. Attempted arrest of Chapman, about to board Cuba boat, but he got away, dropping valise containing $8800 in currency. Will tender resignation on request. DETTERBACH.

"I've already wired Detterbach for his resignation," Vickers said to Fenton. "He shouldn't have taken any chances with Chapman. None of my operators should take chances with him. Understand that, Fenton?"

"Yes, Mr. Vickers," said Fenton soberly. "You're sending me after Jim Chapman?"

"That train gets in to Chicago in an hour. I know Mrs. Chapman by sight. I'll point her out to you and then you follow her. I've a hunch she's going home, to Freedom, Missouri. Chapman will get in touch with her. Maybe in a day or two, maybe not for two or three months. That doesn't matter. You'll stay on the ground."

"In Clay County?"

Vickers nodded. "You'll be selling Bibles. And you'll really be selling them, understand?"

"I sold enough of them before I went to work for you; I suppose I can sell some more."

"Right! That's Bible country, down there. But don't put on any hillbilly clothes. Willie Gibson will be there, as an itinerant photographer. He'll get in touch with you, but you're not to be seen together. You'll be well dressed, a distinct contrast to Willie. The Bibles will be waiting for you at the Dekker Hotel in Kansas City. But take a few samples with you from here. All right, now, I'll meet you at the station. I'll wear a beard and a linen duster; Indiana farmer. Have you got everything?"

"I believe so, Mr. Vickers. I'm to arrest Chapman on sight?"

"Good God, no! Not in Clay County. You'd never get away with him. If you see him, you're to report to the Kansas City office. I've given them instructions. We've got thirty men there and the Federal troops will give us whatever assistance we need. I don't want you to do anything rash and I don't want failure. Understand?"

The train left Chicago at four o'clock and Fenton met Evelyn Chapman three hours later, by simply following her to the dining car and letting events take their natural course. Being late, the car was crowded.

Fenton stepped back into the vestibule until a couple left

the diner. Then he moved forward and saw that Evelyn was being seated at the table just vacated. When the steward returned to the door, Fenton said to him, "Can't you find a table for me? I'm about starved."

"If yo-all don't mind sittin' with someone else?"

"I don't. I'm hungry."

The steward led Fenton to Evelyn's table. Fenton seated himself, studied the menu for a moment or two, then gave his order. Finished with that duty he folded his hands on the table and smiled pleasantly at Evelyn Chapman.

"The weather's fine, it's a long trip and the dining service is terrible," he said brightly. "Shall we go on from there?"

Evelyn looked at him steadily. "Why?"

"Because it's old-fashioned not talking to strangers to whom you haven't been introduced. My name is Tom Fenton and I'm a salesman. I'm going to Kansas City to sell Bibles to the natives of the Ozarks."

"The Ozarks are two hundred miles from Kansas City. Excuse me, I don't think I'll have dinner after all."

Tom Fenton flushed, then pushed back his chair. "I'm sorry," he said stiffly. *"I'll* leave."

Later, he decided that it had been a good move, after all. If she saw him in Freedom, she'd remember him as an impertinent traveling salesman. An abject apology would serve as an introduction. It was better than approaching her cold.

In Kansas City, Fenton went to the Dekker Hotel and found a large parcel awaiting him. He emptied one of his carpetbags of clothing and stuffed it with Bibles.

An inquiry at the hotel desk produced the information that he had to take a coach to Independence and there transfer to the Freedom stage. It was early afternoon when he boarded the Independence coach. Evelyn Chapman was not on the coach. She had either traveled by an earlier one or had made arrangements for a private carriage. Fenton had not seen her after getting off the train in Kansas City. That she had traveled that far indicated plainly enough that she was going home. She would not hide in Freedom.

There were three other passengers on the Independence coach and Fenton carried on a brisk conversation with all of them. He almost sold a Bible to one of the passengers.

When he got off the stage in Independence, Fenton saw a sidewalk photographer near by. Carrying his carpetbags he walked past the photographer.

"Take yer pitcher, Mister," the photographer hailed him.

"On'y twenty-five cents and ye c'n send it to yer sweetie to remember ye by." Willie Gibson was over fifty. He hadn't washed in several days and his clothes looked as if he had slept in them for at least a month. A couple of his teeth were missing in front and when he grinned, as he was doing now, he looked like an oaf.

Fenton paused briefly in his stride. "Sorry, old man, I've had my picture taken."

'On'y twenty-five cents," Willie Gibson urged, "three nice pitchers for a half a dollar." Under his breath he said, "Don't go to Freedom!"

Fenton walked on. At the next corner he stopped and looked back. Willie Gibson was talking earnestly to a stout woman with two children.

Fenton frowned. He'd had his instructions from Alan Vickers himself. Go to Freedom and remain there until you see Jim Chapman, then communicate with the Kansas City office.

There was a livery stable across the street. Fenton went to it. "I'm a traveling salesman," he told the liveryman. "I expect to work between here and Freedom for a few days, perhaps a couple of weeks and I'd like to rent a horse and buggy."

The liveryman looked thoughtfully at Fenton. "You're a stranger, here. I'll have to have a deposit. Twenty-five dollars."

Fenton paid it and a few minutes later, drove a rig out of the stable. He took the road north, out of Independence.

He had cleared the limits of the town when it struck him that he had not seen Willie Gibson and his camera, as he came out of the barn. It was just as well. The old man was a little too skittish for this business. Willie had been a spy for McClellan in the early days of the war. He'd been captured in Richmond and sentenced to death. During the Peninsular Campaign when it looked as if McClellan would crush Joe Johnston's army, the prison guards had been lax and Willie escaped. The experience had left its mark on Willie, however.

He shouldn't really have been in this business. At least not out on the firing line.

Tom Fenton became aware suddenly that a big man was plodding along the side of the road, going in the same direction he was going.

The detective hailed him. "Hi, neighbor! Can I give you a lift?"

He was a clean-shaven fellow in his early twenties. "You sure can give me a lift, stranger," he said, climbing into the buggy beside Fenton. "I'm going on toward Freedom."

"So am I," said Fenton. "You live around Freedom?"

"Uh-huh. Drummer, are you?"

Fenton chuckled. "Brother, I'm selling Heaven. Reach down in that bag and bring out just the finest Bible ever printed, genuine morocco half-leather binding."

"Bibles," said Fenton's passenger. "Alan Vickers is certainly good at figuring things out. First, photographs, and now, Bibles."

"Eh?" said Fenton, as a chill settled over him. "Who is Alan Vickers?"

"Your boss. Take it easy, detective!"

Fenton started to reach for his carpetbag, but the big man kicked his hand away. His own hands remained in his lap. Fenton, shooting a quick glance at the other's face, saw a half-sad smile on the big features. "Stop the buggy around the turn, here."

But it wasn't Fenton who stopped the horse; nor was it the big man beside him. It was a short, heavyset man who got up from a log beside the road.

There was a Navy Colt in his fist. "The old fellow's coming, Clem," he said.

Clem Tancred climbed down from Fenton's buggy. "Better get off, Mister," he said.

Clem caught Fenton's arms as he descended. He held him with one hand and frisked him with the other. He did not touch Fenton's carpetbags in the rig.

In the meantime, the shorter man walked back to the turn in the road and looked in the direction of Freedom. Fenton heard the clop-clop of a horse's hoofs and when the sound came close he could stand it no longer.

"Look out!" he cried. "Look out, Willie!"

Clem Tancred whipped a revolver from under his coat and shot Fenton in the face. At the turn of the road, a revolver cracked twice.

"It's a good thing Jim sent us that telegram that his wife was coming home," said Dick Wood, coming back toward Clem Tancred. "If I hadn't gone to Chicago and rode back on the same train I wouldn't have spotted this detective."

"I don't know," said Clem Tancred, looking down at the dead man at his feet. "Jim won't like this. It's going to make things pretty tough around here."

In Chicago, Alan Vickers stared at the telegram he had just received from Kansas City.

"I warned Fenton to be careful," he whispered. "I warned him. But I'll get Jim Chapman for this. I'll get him if it takes ten years."

Nineteen

IN THE WINTER of 1876, a man named Darlington, who had never been west of Philadelphia, wrote, in *Harper's Magazine,* an article, entiled: "Bad Men of the West." Among other things the article ventured the astonishing assertion that Jim Chapman was not a man at all, but a name applied to many men.

"We know there is a Wild Bill Hickok, because we saw him in Buffalo Bill's Wild West Show. We know there is a Wyatt Earp and Bat Masterson, because these men are actively engaged as peace officers in that Bibulous Babylon of the Plains, Dodge City. We know there are outlaws like Rudabaugh, killers like Clay Allison and John Wesley Hardin, because they have been seen. But who has ever seen Jim Chapman?

"The men he has held up and robbed? Bosh! Robberies there have been—many of them. Trains are held up, banks robbed of fabulous amounts. But who has committed the crimes? Jim Chapman . . . or twenty different men in twenty different localities? Jim Chapman holds up a bank today in Virginia, tomorrow, he robs a train in Iowa and on the same day he is just as liable to be killing a man in Kentucky or shooting up a town in Missouri.

"Is he man or devil, this Jim Chapman? *Or is he merely a legend?*

"Everyone knows that John Wilkes Booth was killed in Virginia in 1865, by Sergeant Boston Corbett. Yet Booth is seen today in Texas. Last year he was in London, England. Tomorrow he is liable to be seen at the opera in New York City. Quantrell, the infamous Confederate guerrilla, was killed in Kentucky, shortly after the war. He crops up every year or two in some outlandish place.

"Consider, then, Jim Chapman. When we were boys we heard about a bandit named Jim Chapman; he robbed the first bank that was ever held up in broad daylight— he stopped and robbed the first train that was ever robbed. Ten years ago we read dime novels around this same Jim Chapman. We grew up on his thrilling adventures. We rode with Jim and Clem Tancred, Hutch Tompkins, Dick Wood and all the others of this band. We fought the Vickers detectives with Chapman.

"We are still riding with Chapman. Alan Vickers is an old man and he is still searching for Chapman. At least, so the newspapers tell us.

"But as for us—we no longer believe the Jim Chapman myth. We don't believe there is—if there ever was—a Jim Chapman. The bottle of milk is missing from a man's doorstep. Who stole it? Why, none other than Jim Chapman.. The Bank of St. Albans, Vermont is robbed of a hundred thousand dollars? Who did it? Jim Chapman.

"A band of Sioux are wiped out in Dakota. Jim Chapman and his band killed them. The next day an isolated settlement is raided—probably by the Sioux in retaliation for the slaughter of their tribesmen, but who is blamed for this second outrage? Jim Chapman.

"To have done one-tenth of the things for which Jim Chapman is blamed, he must be a hundred years old and he must be at least twenty men. All of them devils. . . ."

A hundred years old? Jim Chapman was thirty and it was fourteen years since Lawrence; nine since he had returned from the war, the last Clay County soldier to come in.

Jim Chapman had become a legend. Clem Tancred, more absurdly bookish than ever, brought the magazine article to Chapman and chuckled as the latter read it. "You see, Jim, we're not human beings. We're devils . . . or something."

For a long time after reading the piece in the magazine, Chapman made no comment. When he did remark on it, he said merely, "Maybe they printed it a little too soon."

"How come, Jim?"

Chapman shrugged. "We're long overdue. Our generation has passed us."

"Well," said Clem Tancred, "all I know is that my rheumatism bothers me these cold, damp nights and that I'd just as soon sit by the fire at home and read. Maybe I'll retire after the Northport job."

Clem would not retire. None of them would. They would go on until the end. The legend already spoke of them in the past tense.

Which was as it should be.

Chapman's life was in the past. The only part of it that

had mattered at all had been eight years ago. His marriage to Evelyn.

They rode into Northport, the most formidable band of outlaws ever assembled.

Jim Chapman was the leader of the band. . . . Jim Chapman the legendary outlaw. He had lasted ten years—ten long years. He had started as a boy and now he was a man. He was thirty years old—and looked forty. He weighed 180 pounds and all of it was muscle and bone. The skin was tight on the bones of his face and his eyes were slightly tinged with yellow. They were terrible eyes.

Aeons ago he had approached such a task with trepidation. He had been sick with dread—afraid that something would go wrong and he would be compelled to shoot. Now it was instinct. He walked into danger, like a wolf walking into a kennel of housebroken dogs.

Besides Jim Chapman there was Clem and Dan Tancred, Clark Welker, Ed Sugrue, Hutch Tompkins and Dick Wood. Men with years of horse and revolver work behind them. Each but slightly behind Jim Chapman in degree of desperation.

They rode into Northport, from four different directions, but as they progressed into the town they converged, by careful timing, upon the bank.

The Tancreds reached it first. They tied their horses to the hitchrail in front of the brick building and moved toward the sidewalk just as Sugrue and Tompkins came up to the hitchrail from the north. Simultaneously, Dick Wood and Clark Welker rode up the street from the south. But they remained in the middle of the street, mounted.

Jim Chapman, wearing linen duster and farmer's straw hat, finished tying his horse to the rail fifty feet from the bank. He walked forward, without seeming to see the Tancreds.

He did not nod or speak to them, but they were close upon his heels as he entered the bank.

It was a big bank. There were three tellers at the windows and in an enclosure near by a man in shirt sleeves sat talking to a bank customer. There were five or six people at the various tellers' windows making deposits and withdrawals before the close of business.

Inside the bank the trio of bandits separated. Dan Tancred stopped near the door, Clem walked to the rear of the bank and turned to face the people lined up by the windows. Chapman stepped up to the enclosure.

Chapman brought his hands out of the pockets of his linen duster and there was a Navy Colt in his right fist.

He said in a loud voice, "This is a holdup. No one'll get hurt if you obey orders!"

The guns of the Tancreds, two per man, leaped into their hands and began swinging around, "Everybody down flat on the floor!" Clem Tancred sang out.

A female bank customer screamed and fell in a dead faint. One or two men exclaimed hoarsely. A teller ducked out of sight behind his counter. The cashier in the enclosure, cried out, "My God . . . you can't!"

"Down on the floor!" roared Clem Tancred.

Customers began obeying and then the teller who had ducked out of sight, came up with a sawed-off shotgun in his hands. He was the unknown quantity that was always present in these things.

Chapman swung slightly to the left and his Navy Colt exploded. The teller went back on his haunches; the muzzle of the shotgun went up and blew a hole in the wooden ceiling.

"Don't anyone else try anything," Chapman said in a terrible voice.

A customer on his hands and knees bleated and fainted, falling on the floor on his face, with a peculiarly loud smack.

Chapman vaulted the low railing before him and caught the bank cashier by an arm. "Come on," he snarled.

He pulled the man from his chair, twisted him about and shoved him toward the money cages. As he stamped close behind him, Chapman whipped the inevitable wheat sack from under the linen duster.

"Put it in here—all but the silver!"

The cashier saw the teller lying on his back, blood on his face and he moaned. He took the wheat sack and stumbled up to the cage. It was locked on the inside. He turned a ghastly, frightened face upon Chapman.

Chapman gestured him to the next cage and a trembling teller unlatched it from the inside. He took the sack from his superior and began stuffing money into it.

Crash. The front window of the bank was blasted by a shotgun charge fired from across the street. Shot rattled on the walls and ceilings.

Chapman said, "Hurry!"

The boys outside began shooting methodically. Above the barking of their revolvers, a rifle roared and a heavy slug smacked into the rear wall of the bank, not three feet from Clem Tancred.

Clem said tightly, "Hurry! . . ."

Dan Tancred turned to the street and began shooting through the broken window.

The first teller finished his task and handed the sack to the cashier, who whipped it along to the second teller, already waiting with his cage door open. He scooped his money quickly into the sack.

It was still a pitifully small amount. Chapman said, "The vault."

The shotgun across the street roared again and Dan Tancred winced in pain. "Goddammit!" he swore and began firing out with both hands.

The rifle thundered again and almost instantly another began zinging bullets toward the bank. One ricocheted off the wall and slapped the steel door of the vault with a whang that caused the approaching cashier to cry out in terror. But Chapman was directly behind him.

"Open it up!" he said.

Outside, Clark Welker galloped his horse up to the very edge of the broken window. He leaned over and cried out: "For God's sake, come on fellows! We're finished."

A bullet hit him in the body and he tumbled from the saddle. He fell on hands and knees, picked himself up and plunged into the bits of remaining glass in the window.

Clem Tancred said, "Give it up, Jim. Clark's down!"

The yellow glowed in Chapman's eyes. He stared at the fumbling hands of the cashier on the lock of the vault and he said, "Hurry up and open that!"

A rifle bullet whacked into Clem Tancred's shoulder and he staggered. "I'm hit, Jim!" he gasped. One of his guns clattered to the floor.

Chapman turned to his reeling comrade, the man who had stuck by him these long years, through lean and fat, through hardship—and pursuit. He said, "All right, Clem. . . ."

He tore the wheat sack from the cashier's hands.

"Clear the way, Dan," he said, "we're coming!"

Dan Tancred sprang to the door, spun around and pitched to the floor of the bank. Wounded Clem Tancred saw his brother fall and rushed forward. "Dan!" he cried in a heart-rending voice. "Dan! . . ."

Dan Tancred's eyes were already beginning to glaze. His lips twitched—and a shudder ran through his body.

"Oh, my God!" cried Clem Tancred to the God he had forsaken many years ago.

Chapman touched him on the arm. "Come on, Clem, we've got to go."

Outside, the rest of the outlaw band had assembled in front of the bank. Sugrue was on the wooden sidewalk, his right arm hanging limp at his side. He was shooting with his left and blood was streaming from a ghastly wound in his face.

Hutch Tompkins and Dick Wood were mounted, but Dick's horse had been hit and was plunging madly. Even as Chapman stepped to the sidewalk another bullet brought the horse down. Dick Wood rolled clear, came up to his feet and went down as the shotgun blasted across the street.

The store directly opposite the bank was a hardware store —an arsenal, for it carried a big supply of shooting irons, and somehow a half dozen men had assembled there, armed themselves from the stock and, crouched behind shelter, were pouring a deadly fire upon the outlaws. And there were citizens on the street and in other stores, all firing. There were at least fifty guns against those of the outlaws.

Clem Tancred staggered to his horse, swung up into the saddle and a bullet hit him again. He swayed, but catching hold of the pommel managed to retain his seat. The deadly rifle downed Ed Sugrue.

And then Jim Chapman dropped the wheat sack. His face paler than it had ever been before, he ran swiftly to his horse, fifty feet away. He swung up just as Hutch Tompkins thundered past him.

Clem Tancred's horse came abreast. Chapman let it pass, then turned in his saddle and whipping out his second Navy revolver, began firing at the front of the hardware store. He fired simultaneously with both hands, without conscious aim —guerrilla fashion, as they had fired in the old days when they had charged with reins in their teeth and a blazing Navy revolver in each hand.

The firing from the hardware store decreased . . . stopped. Chapman whirled his horse and sent it galloping after the two horses that had passed him.

A half-grown boy popped out of a drugstore, pointed a rifle at Chapman and pulled the trigger. Fire exploded in his chest, made him gasp with pain. He threw his gun instinctively toward the boy, pressed the trigger and at the last split second jerked up the muzzle. The bullet went feet over the boy's head. And with him standing, gaping at Chapman in awe, Chapman leaned forward in his saddle and rode out of Northport.

He caught up with Hutch and Clem at the end of the street. Hutch had fallen back to ride even with the wounded Clem. By a miracle, Hutch was untouched by bullets.

They were three of seven who had ridden into Northport. They rode out empty-handed and two of them wounded. Behind them was organizing the greatest pursuit and manhunt in history.

"Can you make it, Clem?" Chapman asked as he rode up beside his old companion.

Clem was already gray in the face. He gasped, "I—can—make it!"

Hutch saw the blood that stained the front of Chapman's linen duster. "Jim," he said in a tone of awe. *"You're* hit!"

"It's nothing," said Chapman, even as pain reached down into his very vitals. "Let's ride."

Back in Northport the pursuit was getting under way. Horses were being commandeered and armed men were climbing into the saddle. The telegraph operator was already sending messages to near-by towns and villages. Posses would spring up on all sides. Chapman knew that, he knew too that he and Clem Tancred were dangerously wounded.

Yet—back in Northport remained Dan Tancred, Dick Wood, Ed Sugrue, and Clark Welker.

Chapman said, "We've got to separate, fellows. Take to the woods. We'll never make a getaway on a straight run."

"But you two are hit—bad!" cried Hutch Tompkins. "You'll need me. . . ."

"We won't. You know what's waiting for anyone of us who gets caught. They're too many for us. We all know the rules. Ride, Hutch, ride like hell. They're . . . coming!"

Hutch whirled his horse and saw the mob of galloping horsemen. His eyes snapped with blazing anger.

"Go ahead, Hutch!" Clem Tancred said. "Me—I'm going. . . ." He plunged his horse into the woods, on the left side of the road.

Chapman said, "Good-bye, Hutch!" and drove his horse into the poplars on the right of the road. There was nothing left for Hutch to do then, but to make a run for it. The possemen could see him. Some of them would go after him, some would turn into the woods on the right and some on the left. There were enough men to follow all through, but in the woods Tancred and Chapman had a chance. A fighting chance, for their lives had been spent in that sort of thing. Ten years now—and four years before that.

Twenty

FIFTY FEET into the poplars a blinding streak of pain caused Chapman to gasp and he knew then that the decision was made for him. He slipped from his saddle, slapped his mount on the rump and dove into a clump of brush. Hugging the earth, he listened and heard the animal crashing through the underbrush. But only for a moment. Then the possemen were out on the road, yelling and shouting.

"One of them went in here!"

Then they went plunging into the woods. They made a fearful racket for there were seven or eight of them—and they had tasted blood back there in Northport. They had accounted for four of the most desperate bandits who had ever robbed a dollar. Three more was a cinch.

Their eagerness lost them Jim Chapman. They had seen him dash into the woods, probably heard his horse away ahead. They did not expect to find him skulking under a bush, a scanty fifty feet from the road. They crashed past him, jabbering excitedly.

Chapman waited until they had passed him, then on hands and knees crawled to the very edge of the road. There he rolled into underbrush and stretched out, with his face touching the sweet-smelling earth. Slowly the blood seeped from the wound in his breast and soaked the leaves and ground under him. But he did not move. He could not move.

Within five minutes he heard shooting in the woods on the other side of the road, not spasmodic, but a rising crescendo of gunfire. And then suddenly there were triumphant yells and the shooting stopped.

Clem Tancred had reached the end of the trail.

A sob caught in Chapman's throat. Clem and Dan Tancred, Wood, Sugrue and Welker. They had been with him all these years. The Tancreds and Welker right from the very start.

They brought him out into the road, dropped him on the earth, not twenty feet from where Chapman lay. They discussed the thing as they milled around.

"Which one is this?" someone asked.

"The way he fought, it must be old Jim Chapman himself."

"Damned if I don't believe it!" someone else said.

A fourth snorted. "Nah, none of this bunch belong to Chapman's outfit. They were a bunch of amateurs. Look at what we did in town."

"The hell with you, Oscar," someone retorted. "The Chapman gang ain't so tough. I'll bet you five dollars one of them'll be Jim Chapman himself."

They made bets on it, then, three or four denying that Chapman would be found among the five dead and the others covering the bets. In the middle of it, one of the possemen yelled. "Look—some of the boys are coming back. They must 'a got another!"

Chapman wept. And as he fought the tears, the thing turned out to be true. Horses galloped on the hard-packed earth. A man yelled from a distance, "We got him! . . ."

Poor Hutch Tompkins. He had got out of Northport alive and it had been futile.

Six out of seven. And Jim Chapman lying in the brush, his lifeblood seeping out of his body. In a little while it would be a perfect score. Seven out of seven.

Twenty-one

DEATH DIDN'T come. The possemen brought back Chapman's black gelding. They beat the woods for hours and hours. Citizenry came out of Northport, took back the bodies of Clem Tancred and Hutch Tompkins and returning and bringing more with them, joined those in beating the brush. They always started a little distance inland. They marched and stamped within a dozen feet of where Chapman hid, but did not become vigilant until they were into the woods a way.

Darkness came and torches were lit. The search continued. It kept on until the stars came out and then, a pale half moon. Then finally quiet settled upon the woods. But not on the road. Men galloped and trotted horses up and down; they challenged one another and gossiped.

Then, at last, Jim Chapman dared get up from the ground. His wound had stopped bleeding long ago, the blood having congealed. But pain gripped him in fiery hands, nausea made him vomit. His muscles were like soft rubber. He was absolutely limp.

Only Jim Chapman would have stuck it out. He groped through the forest. Sometimes he fell and crawled for short distances. Sometimes he lay exhausted, gathering strength. His wound bled and stopped bleeding.

Toward morning, he came to a dark, silent little village. He tried to skirt it and found himself in the railroad yards, with a train of boxcars standing upon the tracks. Half delirious, Chapman slunk along the train and found a sealed boxcar. He broke the seal, pulled open the door a couple of feet and crawled into the car.

He closed the door from the inside and in pitch blackness groped about. The car seemed to be about half filled with barrels, wooden boxes and bales wrapped in burlap. He crawled far in among them and then sheer exhaustion overtook him and he went to sleep.

He woke once to feel the train swaying and creaking under him, but he could not rouse himself sufficiently to move.

The next time he regained consciousness it was not so dark in the car. He could see outlines of boxes and barrels and to the sides tiny chinks of light, coming in from outside. The train was still moving.

He pondered that heavily. How long had he been in here? How long had the train been moving? In which direction was it going? Southward? No, that was too much to expect. East or West, then. They would know about it, there, too. They would know about it throughout the country. The Chapman gang completely destroyed, six killed and only one still at large. Ah, they would seek that one. They would ring the country with steel and fire.

The train hooted twice and it seemed to Chapman that it was slackening speed. Good Lord, it was reaching its destination. The trainmen would be coming along and discover the broken seal. They would . . . find Jim Chapman!

Desperately, Chapman scrambled to his feet and found himself so stiff and sore he could scarcely move. But he got to the train door somehow and after terrific effort, forced it open. Green poplar trees rushed past the train. Here and there a clump of silver birch.

Yes, the train was slackening. Chapman plunged out. He saw green-swathed earth rush up to meet him and then blackness exploded and enveloped him in its merciful blanket.

There were long shadows on the ground, when grudging consciousness returned to him this time. He lay for a while looking up at a patch of blue sky. He rolled his head sidewards and saw the sun, big and tinged with red. It was low in the sky; in the west, no doubt. A night and a day had almost passed since Northport.

Chapman was still free, still alive. . . .

He'd beaten them, after all. They had not caught him. They wouldn't now. Chapman knew that. He *felt* it. If it had been his time, they would have had him by now. He had lain here all day, in the open and they had not found him.

They wouldn't. His head was clear, his brain functioned as smoothly as it ever had. His instinct of self-preservation was as strong as ever. He got up from the ground where he had fallen from the train, saw that he was a good twenty feet from the tracks and just beside a solid wall of virgin poplars.

He entered them and moved cautiously in what he judged to be a northward direction. The train had been slackening when he threw himself out. A town was up in that direction and a town meant food. . . . Somehow.

Food Chapman needed. He was horribly weak, battered and

bruised even though the bullet wound merely throbbed dully now. He had to have food, to recoup his strength.

After five minutes of cautious traveling through the poplars, they thinned and he looked out upon a field. He inhaled softly, in pleasure.

Withered, brown plants dotted the field. A potato patch, the potatoes ready in the ground for digging.

But beyond the field was a long cabin, from which smoke came. Chapman crouched down in a clump of brush at the edge of the field and watched the cabin.

After a while a man came out of it, carrying an enameled pail. He went to an enclosure behind the house and remained inside for ten minutes or so. When he came out the pail was heavy. He had milked a cow in there.

The red ball of sun dipped down to the horizon. There were a few minutes of twilight and then the sudden northern darkness fell upon the earth.

And at last, Chapman came out from his hiding place. He went only to the nearest hill of potatoes and crouching, dug them up, one by one, with his fingers.

They were big, smooth potatoes. He wiped the earth from them upon his linen duster and ate the potatoes, raw, his teeth gritting upon the dirt that clung to them. He ate two potatoes, then was violently sick for a few minutes. After a while he ate another, smaller potato and then dug up another hill and stuffed the tubers into the pockets of his duster. He took out his Navy revolver and stuck it into this trousers belt to make more room in the pockets for the potatoes.

Despite a bit of nausea from the raw potatoes he felt better after that and returning to the railroad tracks, walked the ties for a half mile until he saw the lights of the town ahead.

He left the tracks then and went forward cautiously. It was a small town, a bare huddle of buildings. But there was a little red depot by the tracks and upon it a name: *Birch City, Wisconsin.*

Chapman had never heard of Birch City in his life. But he was still in Wisconsin. That knowledge worried him. He'd hoped—well, he'd hoped that the train had taken him far beyond the borders of the state. For not until then could he feel even reasonably safe.

There was a light in the bay window in the front of the little depot. Chapman could see the telegraph operator working his key and heard the clickety-clack of the instrument. There was no one else around the station.

Chapman approached cautiously and risked a quick look into the lighted window of the tiny waiting room. It was empty, but his eyes saw a little rack, containing timetables. He debated the risk with himself for a moment, then drawing a deep breath, walked boldly up to the door of the waiting room, opened it and reaching inside, plucked up one of the timetables. He walked quickly away from the station and did not stop until he was well clear of it.

He found a culvert under the tracks and getting down on his hands and knees, crawled under, splashing in a tiny trickle of water. Well inside, he sat down in the cramped space and fished a match from his pocket.

Spreading open the timetable in the middle, where they habitually carried their maps, he lit the match. He had guessed right—there was a map. But where was Birch City?

He found Northport, saw that the railroad wound north and west. He followed its course, through the dots and names on the map that indicated towns along the railroad. The match burned his fingers and he lit another.

And then he found Birch City. He exclaimed softly. It was almost at the northwestern edge of the state, only two or three stations outside of Superior. It was at least three hundred miles from Northport. So he *had* traveled.

After he considered it for a while, he decided that it was the best thing that had happened for him. They would have been waiting for him down South. They knew that the Chapman gang always headed for Missouri—and sanctuary. They had spread a line of guns all along the southern border of the state and probably on the west and east. They would not have expected him to go north. North there was only wilderness.

Jim Chapman had gone north, however. Without a horse he had traveled three hundred miles in a single night and day.

Twenty-two

ABILENE, KANSAS, in 1867, had been a speck on the prairie. It had set the example for the subsequent boom towns of the west. After Abilene there came Hays, Ellsworth, Wichita, Newton—and Dodge City.

Deadwood, in Dakota Territory passed them all. There was gold in Deadwood. They blasted it from the mountains, dredged it from the streams and they fought and died for it in Deadwood City.

It was the rawest frontier city of them all and there Chapman would be safe until the hue and cry died.

The riffraff that had been in the cattle towns, that had followed the gleaming rails of the Union Pacific from Council Bluffs to Promontory Point in Utah, were at Deadwood. They had brought their friends and cousins. Everything that had been bad in Cheyenne and Dodge, was twice as bad in Deadwood.

Chapman climbed down from the Butterfield stagecoach in front of the Wells Fargo office, which was next door to the Golden Gulch Saloon and Dance Hall.

The Wells Fargo agent rushed anxiously up to the driver. "Make it all right?"

"Yeah, sure," replied the driver. "They musta figured there weren't any capitalists on this trip."

Chapman remarked to a Deadwood citizen on the sidewalk, "They hold up the stages coming *into* Deadwood?"

The citizen spat out tobacco juice. "Yah, bunch of penny-ante stickup artists here. They held up three stages last week and got a total of eleven dollars all told. One of 'em give his name as Jim Chapman. Yah!"

Chapman stiffened. Was there any place where his name wasn't known and bandied about?

He walked into the Golden Gulch Saloon and blinked when he saw the seventy-five-foot bar that stretched down the entire length of the room and was well patronized in the middle of the afternoon.

There were eight bartenders and Chapman had to wait several minutes before he could get a glass of whisky. It cost fifty cents.

"There must be gold in Deadwood after all," he muttered.

A roughly dressed miner next to Chapman nudged him. "There he comes!"

Chapman looked to the door and saw a tall, erect man striding into the saloon. He was dressed in immaculate Prince Albert and silk hat, although his hair was so long it touched his shoulders. It was peculiarly silky hair of a golden color and so wavy it seemed to have been treated with a hot iron. The man had long mustaches to match his hair.

"That's Wild Bill," the man next to him whispered hoarsely.

Chapman watched the man with interest. So this was the man reputed to be the best revolver man in the entire West, the man who was almost a legend himself.

Wild Bill proceeded to the rear of the big saloon and a place was made immediately for him at a faro table. Chapman took note that the place was so selected that Wild Bill's back was to the wall.

A buzz ran through the saloon and men began to move to the rear to observe Wild Bill at his chosen calling of gambling. Chapman moved along with the crowd and finally came to a halt six or seven feet from Wild Bill, almost directly across from him.

The gamblers were playing faro, a game that Chapman was not too familiar with, although it was simple enough. The banker was a sallow, cold-eyed man with abnormally soft, white hands.

There was something familiar about the man, but Chapman could not place him. He was not even sure for that matter that he had ever seen him. It was probably the type that was familiar rather than the individual. He had seen many gamblers.

Wild Bill was a cautious, silent player. He watched the cards come from the banker's box and whenever two of a certain value had come out in favor of the bank, he played the card with a ten-dollar chip. At other times he contented himself with a dollar bet.

It was apparent that Wild Bill's type of playing was not to the banker's liking. He kept searching the faces of the players and the watchers behind and in a dull monotone kept urging others to join in the game.

"Twenty can play as well as one," he droned. "Lay down your bets, gentleman. There are no odds in favor of the bank. Just put your money down and win. . . . Ah, Mr. Hickok wins again! Double your money, sir, and win twice as much."

Wild Bill was heedless of the banker's urging. He put a dollar on the three and another on the king. Chapman turned away from the game . . . and came face to face with the most striking woman he had ever seen in his life.

She was tall and of regal appearance and wearing a green velvet gown. She had the most perfect features of any woman he had ever seen. Her hair was of burnished gold. He stared at her and in the act of greeting him, her eyes widened.

Then Chapman recognized her. She was Vivian Braddock whom he had met years ago in Abilene. Instantly, his head swiveled away from her, to the face of the banker who had seemed familiar.

Of course! It was Wes Braddock!

He turned back to her, his mouth tightening in a thin, straight line.

"Hello," she murmured.

He touched her arm and signaled with his eyes for her to come to one side, away from the crowd. She nodded and led the way, not to the side, but through a door into a private room.

Closing the door behind him, he said, "You know who I am?"

"Of course. I recognized you instantly. You've . . . become pretty famous."

His upper lip curled. "Your husband? . . ."

She shook her head. "He won't remember you, and—he isn't my husband."

"No?"

"He hasn't been since '67. I didn't even see him until I came to Deadwood last fall. He's merely a house player here, like a dozen others."

"You own this place?"

She laughed shortly. "I guess you haven't been around. I made a half million dollars out of the Kansas cattle business. I'm going to retire after Deadwood folds up. I've earned every dollar that I've got in the banks in Chicago and New York."

He looked at her steadily. There was a bitterness—and weariness—in her tone that he had never heard before in anyone else.

He said suddenly, "How old are you, Vivian?"

A half smile crossed her face. "I was exactly nineteen when Wes Braddock walked out on me in Abilene, leaving me without a cent of money and the hotel mortgaged."

"Why," he said, "you're younger than I am."

"And what are you? Thirty? I read an article about you in a magazine last winter in which they called you a legend."

"I read it, too. That was the first time I realized I'd outlived my generation. I almost didn't go to Northport."

Her eyes squinted in sympathy. "It was pretty bad, wasn't it?"

He nodded. "They were my friends."

She was silent a moment, then, "You know that Deadwood is full of rumors? It has been, ever since Northport. There are big bullion shipments going out of here and Wells Fargo has raised its rates sky-high since the rumors started that you were here, waiting for a good chance."

He shook his head quickly. "No. No. I'm through. I'm not here for that. It's just—well, where else can I go? I've been—everywhere."

"And Evelyn Comstock? The girl you married back in '68?"

"That was a mistake."

"Mistake? Yet—" She looked at him sharply, then gave her head a quick shake— "Are you going to stay long in Deadwood?"

"I only got here a half hour ago. It's good. . . . Vivian, it's good to see you. You tried to be a friend to me once."

"I think," she said steadily, "I've been your friend all these years. Sometimes when the chase was getting close, I wished that I hadn't forgotten how to pray. When there was a report that you were in Wichita . . . in Ellsworth or in Dodge, I looked for you—"

She broke off as there was a knock at the door. She looked quickly at Chapman, then called. "What is it?"

Wes Braddock came in. "Wild Bill tapped the bank. I need five hundred."

"Tell Maurice I said it was all right," Vivian Braddock said.

Wes Braddock started out of the office, then turned back. "Haven't I seen you somewhere, stranger?"

"No," Vivian Braddock said curtly. "Mr. Carson has just come from Butte."

Braddock nodded and went out, but Chapman saw that there was still a speculative look in his eyes. He said, "He may remember."

"No, I don't think so. You were just a boy in Abilene. I

remembered you from your eyes. Braddock isn't that sharp. Just remember the name I gave you. Carson."

"All right. I'll make it Sam Carson. I've never used that name."

"Good. And—my name is Vivian Morgan. It was that before I married Braddock. Well, Sam Carson, get yourself a room at the Deadwood Hotel. And don't leave suddenly, without seeing me first."

He nodded. "What's the situation here?"

"You mean law? Nothing to speak of. A sheriff, a couple of town marshals and a U.S. deputy marshal. Not your caliber at all."

"Wild Bill?"

"Strictly what you saw out there. He did the same in Abilene except he wore a badge and drew down wages on the side. Bat Masterson was here for a while, but he's gone back to Dodge. You'll run into Wyatt Earp. He rides shotgun on the stage, but they advertise it every time he starts out. There are some small-time Texas boys here, who may amount to something someday. Look them over. Their names are Joel Collins and Sam Bass. They may have been starved out, though. I haven't seen them in a week."

Chapman left the Golden Gulch Saloon and hunted for the Deadwood Hotel. It was in the next block, a three-story building of unpainted lumber with cracks a half-inch wide, between the boards. Some of the cracks were chinked with moss, some with mud mixed with grass. It got cold here in winter.

He bought a copy of the local newspaper published by an enterprising pioneer and the first thing he saw in it was his name.

IS JIM CHAPMAN IN DEADWOOD?

The paper asked that question and below the two-column head recounted the various rumors already related to Chapman by Vivian Morgan. The reporter touched on the Northport affair and went so far as to intimate that Jim Chapman was one of the three unidentified dead. Relatives of the Tancreds and Dick Wood had come up to Northport and identified them, but the bodies of Hutch, Ed and Clark Welker had been buried without names. No photographs of Jim Chapman had ever existed and no one even knew what he looked like.

Alan Vickers could have told them. But the name of Vickers was in nowise connected with the Northport affair. Vickers was an institution, not a man. The new generation no longer thought of the Vickers Detective Agency as one man any more than they thought of the Union Pacific Railroad as an individual. Times had changed.

Chapman stretched out on the cot in his narrow room and for the first time in three weeks fell into a dreamless, restful sleep. He awoke once when it was dark, but did not bother to get up and undress. He had slept too many nights with all his clothes on.

Twenty-three

IN THE MORNING the sun was shining and he went out to see Deadwood. The streets were sparsely populated and he spent a half hour walking briskly about.

Hungry, then, he went into a large restaurant next to the Deadwood Hotel and ordered breakfast. As he sat waiting for the food to be cooked, Wild Bill came in with a big somber man.

They seated themselves at the table next to Chapman's, ordered ham and eggs and conversed in low, quiet tones. Chapman with his elbow almost touching Wild Bill's heard him say, "I tell you, Wyatt, I wasn't going to come to this town. My luck had run out and I had the strangest feeling about Deadwood that I've ever had. But now, I don't know. I won yesterday, for the first time. A lot. If my streak holds for another week or two I'm going back to Cincinnati with a stake."

The somber man nodded. "This town's worse than Dodge ever was. The cowboys drink a lot and do a lot of shouting, but you know how they're going to act, because they all do the same thing. But here, Bill—there are too many sharpers. You've got to watch them all the time."

Wild Bill stroked his golden mustache. "That's right. I wouldn't even be surprised if Chapman *is* here. Did you ever run across him?"

The man called Wyatt shrugged. "There was a fellow in Wichita two years ago I suspected. He had a big chap for a partner, who could have been Clem Tancred. They stayed a week then went off. No one ever did learn their names . . . or business."

The waitress brought Chapman's food and he began to eat. After a while, he was aware that Wild Bill had turned his chair slightly and was watching him. He looked up and nodded.

"How do you do, Mr. Hickok."

Wild Bill's eyes narrowed suspiciously, but he bobbed his head curtly. "You were watching the game yesterday."

"That's right. Vivian Morgan is an old friend."

"Yes? Remarkable woman. . . . This is my friend, Mr. Earp, from Dodge."

Chapman acknowledged the acquaintance with a smile. "My name is Sam Carson. I'm from Texas by way of Virginia City and Butte."

"Ah, a mining man," said Wyatt Earp.

"Yes, but I came to Deadwood too late. All the worthwhile claims are taken."

Earp nodded in agreement. "I found the same thing true. The capitalists will soon have everything around here. I may go back to Dodge."

"I've thought of visiting there," said Chapman. "Is it—like they say?"

"We've tamed her," said Wyatt Earp calmly.

Chapman turned to Wild Bill. "My brother was in Abilene for a short spell."

"Yes?" Wild Bill said sharply.

"But that was in '72," Chapman said. "After the drovers stopped going there."

He finished the last of his coffee and got up. "Good morning, gentlemen. I may see you in a game later."

He went back to the hotel and the clerk called to him. "Mr. Carson, there's a message for you."

Chapman took the envelope and ripped it open. The message was from Vivian Morgan and it asked him to come and see her as soon as he could.

He walked to the Golden Gulch and early as it was, found her in her office. Her face was strained and she looked older than she had the day before.

"I do a lot of business with Wells Fargo," she said. "Handy, the agent, told me—in confidence—that Alan Vickers is here."

Chapman looked at her steadily and she went on quickly, "His agency has represented the company for years, but you know—he isn't here for that reason. It's the rumors. . . ."

"Where would he be? The hotel?"

"He's next door right now. Handy left to meet him. I suppose . . . you'll be going, now?"

He sighed wearily. "I suppose. I always have."

"Where to this time?"

"There aren't many places left. I don't know."

"You have money?"

He nodded. "Thanks. I guess this is good-bye—again."

When he was at the door, she spoke. "I'll close up here. I've had enough."

He turned. "You guessed it yesterday, Vivian. Besides, the sand's running out pretty fast." He bent his head and went out.

When he neared the door of the almost deserted saloon, two men came in. One was an enormously fat man with iron-gray hair and a smoothly shaven face. He had snow-white shaggy eyebrows and piercing, steely eyes.

He and Chapman stopped at the same time, then the fat man said to the man with him, "Go back to the office. I'll talk to you later."

He walked to the side of the saloon, away from the bar and Chapman followed him. They looked at one another, then sat down at the table.

"Well, Jim," Alan Vickers said. "It's been a long time."

"You've put on a little weight," Chapman remarked.

Vickers eyes flashed. "And white hairs. I'm fifty-four and I look sixty-five. You almost ruined me back there in '68 when I lost the railroad contracts. Fortunately Philip Castlemon tided me over—remember Philip?"

"Of course. How is he?"

"Philip sent a bullet through his head, six years ago. He had T.B." Vickers grunted as he saw Chapman's face. "You *do* feel!"

"Not much . . . since Northport. What is this, Alan?"

Vickers spread out his big hands and looked at them. "That's up to you, Jim."

"I only know one way."

Vickers' eyes glinted. "It has to be that way. Oh . . . *I'm* too old. Don't worry. But my man who went out. . . ."

Chapman pushed back his chair. He looked down at Vickers, his nostrils distended. "You knew?"

"Of course. Remember what I told—" He broke off.

Wes Braddock, his face flushed from early morning drinking, came unsteadily into the saloon. He saw Vickers and Chapman and swerved in their direction. He let his right hand dangle at his side and shook his arm as he approached.

He said thickly, "You found him, Vickers. I told you I was sure. He thought I didn't remember. . . ."

"Braddock," said Chapman, "you ran out on me in Abilene. If it hadn't been for that money. . . ."

Braddock sneered. "Fifty thousand dollars, Vickers. Mine . . . mine alone. . . ." He shook his right arm again and a double-barreled .41 derringer fell from his sleeve into his palm.

He was too drunk even then, to get in the first shot. Chapman's hand shot under his brown sackcloth coat, came out and the Navy Colt roared before Braddock had the derringer even with his waist.

The bullet smashed Braddock back over a table and it crashed to the floor with him. Chapman did not even look. His eyes remained on Vickers.

The famous detective, gray and old, sat waiting for it. His face was set.

"I guess I should," Chapman said softly, "but—"

"You may be sorry," Vickers said unyieldingly.

A couple of men were looking in at the door. One of the three morning bartenders laid a Frontier Model across the bar and seemed uncertain about it. His hand shook.

"Wait!"

Vivian Morgan's voice rang out from the doorway of her office. She pointed at the bartender with the gun. "Put that away."

The bartender shook himself. "He just shot Braddock. I'd bet—"

"Put it away!" snapped Chapman. "I don't want to kill you. . . ."

"Let him have it," cried Alan Vickers. "He's Jim Chapman!"

The bartender dropped the Frontier Model on the bar and recoiled in horror.

"This way, Jim!" said Vivian.

He walked sidewards toward her. They were crowding at the front door now and some of them had guns in their hands. Alan Vickers struggled from his chair and appealed to them.

"Get him! He just killed a man and he's Jim Chapman. There's fifty thousand dollars reward. . . ."

A rumble began out on the sidewalk and the sudden push spilled men into the saloon; frightened men who suddenly wanted more than anything in the world to be outside— pushing, with other men in front of them.

Chapman thought he caught a glimpse of long golden hair and his teeth parted in a grim smile. Still walking methodically he reached Vivian's side.

She tried to step behind him to shield him as he passed through the door, but he threw out his left hand and held her away.

"Hurry!" she said desperately. "They'll have their nerve in a minute. . . . Go straight through the rear door. You'll find some horses out there. Get the black. . . ."

At the front door someone yelled and a gun thundered.

"Go!" Vivian screamed in terror. She shoved at him with both hands.

He tried to pull her around ahead of him and then the bullet slammed her body against him. The force of it sent them both into her office. She was still pushing against him.

"Hurry . . . hurry . . . hur—" The strength went out of her. He kicked the office door shut and regardless of bullets that whipped through the thin panels, stooped and put her on the floor.

"Oh . . ." she said. "You . . ." Blood gushed from her mouth and she was dead.

Instinct alone got Chapman to his feet again. Instinct, nurtured by ten years of flight. He moved swiftly to the back door, tore it open and then took a last look before plunging outside.

The horses were as she had told him. Only they were unsaddled. But that made no difference to Chapman. He leaped upon the back of the black and was off.

Flight, of course, was second nature to him. He was the master of them all in that art. A good horse under his legs and a revolver in his belt and no man on earth could catch him. They'd never get Chapman that way. He had survived even Northport.

Two days south and east of Ogallala, Chapman came suddenly upon two travelers. He had not cut their trail, but topping a small rise he rode down into a coulee and there they were hunkered down over a tiny fire of buffalo chips, cooking a meal.

It was too late for Chapman to retreat. He had to bluff it out. Hands held loosely at his side, he let his mount pick its way down to the camp.

Both men rose and faced him. Chapman noted that the thumbs of one were hooked in his wide cartridge belt. He said,

"Howdy, stranger."

"Saw your fire," Chapman said disarmingly.

"You *saw* it?" one of the men asked, accenting the word.

Chapman knew then that they had camped in the coulee purposely, so that no one would see their fire. He smiled.

"Smelled it."

The man who held his hands hooked in his belt relaxed. He even held out his right hand to Chapman. "My name's Bass, Mister. Sam Bass."

His companion gave him a quick scowl. "My name is John Smith."

Chapman dismounted and shook hands with them. "I'm John Simmons. That buffalo hump smells mighty good. Been up to the hills?"

The eyes of John Smith narrowed, but Sam Bass chuckled. "I'm probably the only man who ever went to a gold camp heeled and went broke there. I had eight thousand dollars when I landed in Deadwood; I left with a dollar and a half and—I robbed that!"

"Sam!" exclaimed Bass' partner.

"Hell," laughed Sam Bass, "he knows we're on the dodge. What's the difference?"

"Come to think of it," said Chapman. "I did hear your name in Deadwood."

"Sure. We held up a flock of stages. Never saw so many poor travelers in my life. Most we ever got from one stage was eleven dollars. And another—I lost a dollar on the deal, giving the poor fellas money for their breakfasts."

"You're a fool, Sam Bass," said the man who called himself John Smith.

"But I'm havin' a good time," retorted Sam Bass. "And once I get back to Texas I'll be all right. I'll get me another good horse and clean up." He grinned at Chapman. "Used to have a mare. Didn't look like nothin' your ever saw, but Mister, she could run. I had a gelding, too. Looked fine, but wasn't anything special. I'd ride the gelding into a place and have my pack on the mare. I'd talk big about the gelding and say he could beat anything the natives could bring out. They'd bring out their best and I'd say, shucks that horse wasn't anything, why my pack horse could even beat it. So they'd look over my mare and then lay me big odds. . . ." A faraway look came into Sam Bass' eyes. "Mister, how that little mare could run!"

"You should have kept her," Chapman said.

"Man shot her. That's why I had to leave Texas. I killed him."

"And they'll be waiting for you when you get back to Texas," said John Smith. "You're a fool, Sam Bass."

"Don't call me that too often," Sam Bass said gently.

Smith looked at Sam Bass, then stooped to his cooking. Bass laughed.

"You're welcome to supper, Simmons, but I'm warning you it might be healthier for you not to travel with us."

They wouldn't chase a man a thousand miles for an eleven-dollar stage robbery. But they knew that Chapman's friends had died at Northport, that he had been alone at Deadwood. They'd be looking for a lone traveler, a man who would shy from casual acquaintances.

Chapman said, "If you don't mind, I'd like to ride with you a ways. Maybe as far as Kansas. It's lonesome on the prairie."

"Sure," said Bass.

"No," Smith said.

"It's all right," Bass laughed, "but if you're a law-man, remember what I told you about Texas."

Chapman nodded. What he meant was that he would just as soon be hanged in Nebraska as Texas, that you couldn't hang a man any deader for two killings than one.

Chapman ate supper with the two men who were on the dodge. Afterwards, Sam Bass brought out a harmonica and played for an hour. Chapman sat on the ground with his arms about his knees and stared into the tiny fire.

When Bass put away his harmonica, he said, "Simmons, I noticed you didn't have any blankets. Better use part of mine."

Chapman shrugged assent. "I didn't make any money in Deadwood, either, but I was broke when I went there."

But Chapman couldn't sleep. He looked at the stars and thought of—Missouri. There were voices in his ears. Clem Tancred said, "I'm going to retire. I'd like to read my books and the rheumatism is bothering me."

Hutch Tompkins said, "Whatever you say, Jim." He had always followed Chapman blindly. And Chapman had led him to Northport.

Ed Sugrue whispered, "It don't look good to me, Jim. I think I saw a Vickers man yesterday." Sugrue had always seen Vickers men. Sometimes they had actually been there.

Chapman closed his eyes and then his ears became more sensitive. He heard horses' hoofs, more than he should have heard. He nudged Sam Bass.

"Someone's coming!"

"Whatsamatter?" mumbled Bass, half asleep.

Across the fire, John Smith sat up suddenly. "Sam!" he whispered hoarsely.

The horses were on the crest of the coulee. The riders were preparing for a quick charge down. Chapman rolled clear of Sam Bass' blanket and crouching, ran for his hobbled horse, near by.

Streaks of fire lanced the darkness and the coulee rang to the roar and whine of rifles and revolvers. Chapman gained his horse, unhobbled it and swung into the saddle. His guns came naturally into his hands and be began firing methodically at the possemen who were coming downhill.

Someone near by screamed in pain. Chapman, in flight, whirled his horse back and rode directly toward the little campfire. Sam Bass sprang up from the ground.

"They got Smith," he cried. "Beat it, Simmons, this is no fight of yours."

"Get up, Bass," Chapman ordered. He sat erect in the saddle and fired steadily at the disorganized attackers.

Sam Bass, however, refused Chapman's invitation to get up behind him. He scudded for his horse, fifty feet away. Chapman followed him, his deadly fire driving off the attackers.

Bass got into the saddle, whooped and charged up the coulee. Chapman was compelled to follow him and the advance broke up the attack completely.

Then Bass and Chapman fled. The possemen would follow, of course. They would organize and probably pick up more men. You couldn't lose a trail on this prairie if you were in a hurry.

After a while, when they had pulled up their horses to a swift walk, Sam Bass said to Chapman, "I warned you not to travel with me, Simmons, but I forgot to tell you why. Me and the boys stuck up the Union Pacific night before last. We got seventy thousand in gold coin. There were seven of us, but we split. That's why I had to get my horse. My split is in the saddle bags." He laughed. "I suppose they figured it was Jim Chapman who pulled the job. That's why they were so skittish about riding down."

Sam Bass laughed again. He saw humor in everything, even in being mistaken for Jim Chapman. There was no use telling him. Sam Bass had gone too far.

Twenty-four

ALAN VICKERS was a broken man. For ten years he had fought a war with Jim Chapman and for ten years Jim Chapman had beaten him. Vickers, who had branches in five foreign countries and correspondents in a dozen others, who had offices in the principal cities of the United States, had been bested by an outlaw, who at his best had only six followers. And now he didn't even have those.

At the beginning Vickers had actually liked the youthful outlaw. Why, he had offered him a job. Had Chapman taken it, no telling where he might have gone. Vickers had no family; he could have passed his vast business on to a younger man, like Chapman.

He remembered that poker game in Chicago. Chapman, but a boy, with a few dollars in his pocket—a boy already on the dodge—had seated himself in a game with a quartet of the shrewdest, most ruthless exponents of the art. Chapman hadn't dribbled along in the game, waiting for a lucky break. No—he plunged with the very first hand dealt him and had backed it to the limit—against Pomeroy, the banker. Pomeroy who could have risked fifty thousand on the turn of a card.

Vickers had chuckled about it. Sure, Jim Chapman had jumped across the line, but hadn't he been driven into it? Vickers had gone to Western Missouri himself. He had observed conditions there and he remembered the first time he had met Chapman—when the boy, still suffering from a wound, had backed down that Union ruffian and his gang. There'd been stories, too, that Pike had been responsible for Chapman's active plunge into outlawry. Vickers had been willing to believe it. And at that stage of the game, he would have risked a lot to help Chapman. Even later—a year later—it hadn't been too late. He'd offered the boy a comparatively easy penance. Ten years. Chapman would have been out now.

Then the years piling up. Chapman had actually forced Vickers to the brink of ruin. Only frantic scrambling on Vickers' part had pulled him out of that. After that, of course, it was war.

Vickers had prosecuted the war with vigor. He had spent a fortune on it. And he had not won one trick. Fenton and

Gibson had died. And those other two in Tennessee—Potter and Downing. . . .

Vickers was the greatest detective in the world. But he had been at it twenty-five years and he was tired. He had grown prematurely old. He wanted to step out of it, sit down by a fire with his pipe. He had only a few years left. But he couldn't enjoy those years knowing that he had been defeated.

He had to win before he could sit down by that fire. He had to get Jim Chapman.

He'd almost got him in Deadwood. It had been split seconds. An instant when his own life had hung in the balance and another instant when victory could have been won.

When it was over, Vickers, shaken and ill, went back to the express office and arranged for passage out of Deadwood. There was no use to stay here now. The wolf had eluded the trap.

Before he left Deadwood, however, he made a final effort. This was the last stab.

He looked up a man who was almost as famous in his own line, as Vickers and Chapman were in theirs. He said to the man, "He's five hundred miles from civilization. He'll be out in the open for weeks. It's a job for a scout and tracker. And a man who knows guns better than Chapman does. I'll pay . . ." He mentioned a sum that made the other man's eyes widen. Yet, after a moment, the man shook his head.

"I could use that sort of money, and I'm not afraid. But I was just married before I came to Deadwood . . . and it wouldn't be right to her to risk it. Not so soon."

Vickers bowed in despair. "Then I can't hire anyone to do it. I've got to do it myself. . . ."

He was ill before he reached Fargo and, on the train going to Minneapolis, he did not care even about Jim Chapman. Then, leaving Minneapolis, he felt somewhat better and had dinner on the train. The porter brought him a Chicago newspaper.

There was a rehash of the whole sordid affair. Vickers was about to throw the paper away when something caught his eye. It was a short paragraph, near the end of the story. It read:

"This was the first time anyone guessed there was another woman, other than the wife he married and deserted, nine years ago. The wife of Jim Chapman, strangely, never divorced him. She is living today in

Clay County, Missouri, not a mile from the place where
Chapman was born. . . ."

Vickers stared at the item for a long moment, then he
suddenly called to the porter, "Bring me some telegraph blanks
—Quick!"

A few minutes later he wrote, a glint in his eyes. Finished,
he reread the telegrams and muttered under his breath. "I've
been a fool to chase him all around the world. I should have
made him come to me. This is the way to do it. I'll bring him
to *my* battlefield."

Twenty-five

THE CIRCLE was growing smaller. Alan Vickers had taken the field himself and he had thrown the personnel and resources of a great industry into the chase. As far away as Cheyenne, Chapman's black horse was the object of scrutiny and he was compelled to desert the animal and steal another at an outlying ranch house.

At Ogallala, Nebraska, he bought a newspaper, a week-old Kansas City *Star*. Chapman always read this paper when he could obtain it, for it was his "home" paper. The item was on page 1 and it received more prominence than it should have received.

Chapman read it and was colder than he should have been even here on the wind-swept Nebraska plateau. It said:

OUTLAW'S WIFE DENOUNCES CHAPMAN

Mrs. Evelyn Comstock (Jim) Chapman in a statement today denounced her husband and said she was filing suit for a divorce. "I was loyal to him," Mrs. Chapman said, "I was loyal and faithful for ten years. I did not believe that he did all the things for which he was blamed. But this Deadwood affair has disillusioned me. I never believed that Jim would take up with a notorious honkytonk woman, while I waited here for him. . . ."

Those were Mrs. Chapman's words to this reporter, but she did not add that there would be an early remarriage, after the divorce; remarriage, that is, for Mrs. Chapman. In Clay County it is rumored that a certain public official has been a frequent caller at Mrs. Chapman's home. . . .

Days later, Chapman rode completely about Lawrence and that night shadowy figures of the past paraded past his campfire. The pirate-bearded, mad-eyed Bloody Bill Anderson, the deadly towhead Quantrell, the diabolic fiend, Todd. And the boys who had become men—Clem Tancred, Hutch Tompkins, Clark Welker . . .

He walked into Kansas City, having ferried across the river a few miles below, after turning loose his horse on the Old Santa Fe Trail.

Crossing the Little Blue and striking out on the Independence Road he was picked up by a bearded German who gave him a lift into Independence. The man could speak only a few words of English, which suited Chapman well.

And then, at last, he was in the thinning brush. The fields were larger today, the brush between the farms not so thick. The war was eleven years in the past and the wounds were beginning to heal.

When the twilight dimmed the brush and the night blacked out the twilight, a chill settled upon Chapman. He knew that he was alone in the woods and not alone. Ghosts walked with him. The ghosts of the long years; ghosts whose mortal bodies were buried far north in alien soil. Chapman had led them there—and he was returning alone.

He passed near a cabin in which a light shone and a dog rushed toward him, barking, then turned suddenly and with tail between his legs, ran howling, back the way he had come.

Chapman laughed and the laugh caught in his throat and sounded strangely like a sob. The moon came out and showed him the road and the lane that turned to the left. A light winked between the trees and he left the lane and cut toward it.

He had not been here in more than nine years. An extra room had been built on to the rear of the cabin and when he walked around it, he hesitated in his choice of the two doors. Finally he decided upon the old one.

He knocked on the door and then stepped quickly back out of the light that would fall upon the ground when the door was opened.

A voice inside called, "Who is it?"

Chapman whistled softly.

There was sudden bustling inside and the door was thrown open. "All right?" Chapman called.

"Jim, for God's sake!" Ed Taylor said hoarsely.

Chapman went in and gripped his brother-in-law's arm. Beyond, Anne got up from a rocking chair. She was heavy and older—much older. She wiped a strand of hair from her strained, pale face.

"Jim."

He could not even kiss or embrace her. All that was too far away. Inanely he said, "Can I rest a minute?"

Anne sobbed so suddenly that a small, four-year-old girl

who had been concealed behind Anne, burst into a loud wail.

Chapman said crookedly, "I haven't seen this one—" He stopped. From the added bedroom came two boys; one tall as a stalk of corn, and almost as thin. He looked vaguely like someone Chapman had known years ago. The older boy was nine or ten.

"Boys," said Ed Taylor, "This is your uncle, Jim. . . ."

Their eyes were wide. The younger boy seemed to shrink behind his brother, but the tall, straight youth came forward. "Uncle . . . Jim Chapman!" he said in a tone of awe.

The little girl howled in fright and Chapman turned toward her. He was not aware of the tragic expression on his face. And then his sister said, "Don't cry, darling. This is your Uncle Jim, come to visit you. . . . Ki-kiss your uncle, Evelyn." Evelyn. . . .

Chapman straightened as if an invisible fist had struck him in the face. "Evelyn," he whispered.

The oldest boy said, "She's named after Aunt Evelyn. . . ."

Ed came up behind Chapman and patted his shoulder. "Sit down, Jim, old man. It's—it's all right. Anne . . . perhaps Jim is hungry."

Chapman winced at the celerity with which his sister grasped her husband's statement. Food she understood. Cooking gave her time to collect her wits, enabled her to keep from looking at him.

The little girl stopped crying, but rubbed her eyes with her little fists and stared at Chapman. The boys dispersed themselves about the kitchen, but after a moment caught their father's eye and disappeared back into their bedroom.

Ed Taylor moved around to the windows and pulled the shades at one or two of them down another half inch or so, although they were already touching the sills. Finally, he came and sat in the rocking chair that Anne had vacated.

"It's been a long time, Jim," he said.

Chapman nodded. Why had he come here? Had the circle narrowed so much that this was the only place left for him—where he had begun?

He could have been in New Orleans by now; New York, or even San Francisco, by that same train—that he had robbed . . . was it three or four times?

Ed was old. He even had a paunch. He must be around thirty-five now, but anyone else would have taken him for forty. Perhaps more.

A long two-tined fork in her hand, Anne turned from the stove. "When did you get here, Jim?"

"Only this evening. I—I've been traveling a lot."

"From Deadwood?"

He started. "You know?"

"Of course we know. Don't we know everything you do? We get newspapers. . . . The woman in Deadwood, Jim? . . ."

He shook his head. "I met her once years ago. She was a fine woman, but—there has never been any woman. Never, Anne. . . ."

He denied it and his eyes were on the child who bore her name. Anne turned back to the stove and said, "Why did you stay away all these years? The others . . . I mean—"

Ed Taylor cut in. "She's a fine woman. She . . . never married again."

There, it was out.

The tiny spark deep in his heart glowed red and burned in the dead, dead tissues. Chapman got up from the chair and took a quick half turn about the kitchen. The face of the older boy, Tommy—he still didn't know the younger one's name—looked out of the bedroom for an instant and with a shock, Chapman knew why he had looked familiar.

Chapman had seen that face. Years and years ago. In cracked mirrors, in still water over which he leaned before dipping his hands. The boy's face was his own, sixteen years ago.

Shivering a little, he turned to Ed who had been watching him. His brother-in-law nodded. "He looks like you, Jim. . . ."

Anne whirled, a terrified expression on her face. "No," she cried. "He looks like my brother, Tom."

"Of course," Chapman said. "I was just going to remark on that." Wind fanned the little flame and it burned higher.

Anne put dishes on the scrubbed kitchen table and poured coffee. Chapman moved up a chair and ate corn pone and fried pork. The food was tasteless, but he lingered over it, because of the words he would have to say when he finished.

When he could delay no longer, however, he pushed back his chair and got up. Ed was sitting in the rocking chair and Anne was standing by the stove. The little girl—Evelyn—sat in a corner on a footstool, regarding him wide-eyed. Her face was tear-stained.

He moistened his lips with his tongue and knew that his nostrils were dilated. Deliberately he said, "Well, I guess I'll have to . . . go, now."

He saw the shudder run through his sister. He walked toward the back door and she sobbed. "You can't go like that, Jim. You're—my brother!"

"Stay here, Jim," Ed said. "It's all right. No one's bothered us in years. There's a bed upstairs and it's cold out tonight."

Without another word, Chapman went to the ladder and climbed up into the loft. He groped for the bed in the darkness and stretched out on it. But not to sleep.

The light in the square hole of the floor went out after a while and he heard his brother's family going to their beds downstairs.

In the far gable there were round holes cut in the boards. For ventilation, Chapman had said when he had cut them ten years ago. A faint light from the moon outside came through the holes and after a while he saw the faces.

They were familiar faces. He had seen them on the wind-swept plateaus of Wyoming, in the Stygian darkness of the forest; yes, even in the caves where he had at times crawled like a beast.

Tonight he saw a new face. He had almost forgotten it in the years. He saw the tints in her cheeks, the light in her eyes. And he saw the light die and the face grow sad. Then the face faded and he could not bring it back again.

He rose up on his elbow and the warning bell rang in his brain. The outlaw's bell that tolled when danger was near. "No," he whispered in the darkness and got up and crept to the hole in the gable.

He put his face to it.

Did a shadow flit across the grass, out there on the ground? Was that a moving shadow at the edge of the brush? It was, of course. Chapman knew these shadows.

He went back to the hole in the floor and descended the ladder. When he touched the floor, a board creaked and he heard movement in the front room.

"Jim?" called his brother-in-law.

They would hear outside, if any of them were close. Cold air blew on the back of Chapman's neck. He crouched to the floor and whispered as only the hunted man could whisper.

"Yes, Ed. . . ."

Ed knew. He didn't put on a light, but he came out in his bare feet. A Winchester repeating rifle was in his hands.

Chapman exclaimed softly. "No, Ed. I'll go!"

"You can't, Jim. They'll shoot you down. They—must know."

"I guess they do. I shouldn't have come here. . . ."

"But we didn't see anyone around. I swear—"

Outside a voice thundered: "Come out, Jim Chapman! We've got the house surrounded."

This, then, was it!

Chapman took the Navy revolver from his belt. "Go back to bed, Ed. No use your—"

The night was split by the roar of a locomotive hurtling the tracks. Flame from outside lit up the room like jagged lightning. Bullets crashed and splintered through the walls.

Chapman slammed Ed to the floor, scuttled to the door and cried. "Stop shooting, I'll surrender, you fools. . . ."

The long thunder rolled louder than before. Hoofs pounded the hard earth outside and the whine and snap of rifles and revolvers was dulled by the boom of shotguns and the fierce yells of maddened men.

They riddled the house from front to back, galloped around it and poured it in from all sides.

The little girl in the other room cried out in absolute terror. Anne sobbed and moaned. From the bedroom burst young Tom Taylor. There was a huge dragoon pistol in his hand. "Come on, Uncle Jim!" he cried. "Let's give them hell!"

Chapman gasped and choked. Acting instinctively, he catapulted up from the floor, snatched the pistol from the boy's hand and dropping it to the floor rocked Tommy's face with the palm of his hand.

Tommy was himself sixteen years ago. But he wouldn't be Jim Chapman of today.

Chapman whirled and rushed to the door. Slamming back the bolt, he jerked the door wide and leaped out into the moonlight.

"Here I am!" he roared.

But it was too late. They had riddled the house like a sieve, they had charged and circled it . . . and then their nerves had broken. Already they were shadows melting into the brush, hoofs pounding away.

Chapman stood in the moonlight, cold sweat bathing him from head to foot. . . . This wasn't the end—yet!

Sobbing behind him, young Tommy Taylor came to the door. "They're running," he said. "Look at them run, the yellow—"

Chapman turned and slapped the boy's face again. Ed Taylor saw and heard and nodded. His hand to his face, the boy stared at Chapman for a moment, then whimpering, turned and went into the house.

"That was fine, Jim," said Ed.

"He's not going to be like me. He can't—"

"I know. He's heard so much about you. We were afraid, Anne and I."

"Send him away," cried Chapman. "Tell him what I really am. A murderer and a thief. A coward who was so afraid of life, he—" He broke off and ran across the moon-bathed grass to the brush.

Twenty-six

IN THE OFFICES of the Vickers Detective Agency on Troost Street, in Kansas City, the detectives watched the old lion march up and down. The faces of the detectives were taut, their eyes smoldering.

"You call yourselves Vickers men?" Alan Vickers lashed at them. "A Vickers man is a detective. He goes where the devil's afraid to go. There was a Vickers man at Appomattox. There was one at Vicksburg and one—" Vickers stopped and glowered at one of them. "*You* were at Vicksburg, Captain Ash. That was why I made you superintendent of the Kansas City branch."

"All right," said Captain Ash, tall and gray. "You can take your badge and—"

"I won't take it!" snapped Alan Vickers. "I won't accept any of your resignations. Not a man of you is going to run out on me. Not now. The time's past for that. I wanted to retire myself—five years ago. And I couldn't. I couldn't retire because there was a case on the books that hadn't been closed out."

He stopped and his eyes snapped from one man to another. "Jim Chapman is the only man who ever licked the Vickers Agency. He's licked us for ten years. Look at the score. We got that loud-mouth amateur bad man, back in '67. I don't even remember his name. We got him because he was the weakest one of the lot—recruited—when Chapman was just a boy. And what have we got since then? Not one of them. A bunch of farmers—" Vickers swallowed hard—"a bunch of farmers up in Wisconsin got six of them. The Tancreds, Tompkins, Welker—men almost as good as Chapman. And we—we got the world laughing at us too. I got him at Deadwood, and he made a fool of me and then—then, at last, when we had him dead to rights, last night when you had only to take his hide and nail it to the wall, you funked it. You, Captain Ash, the best man I've got in the agency and the rest of you—picked men, all of you. You surrounded Jim Chapman in his own home and you let him get away. . . ."

Captain Ash muttered and looked desperately at his operators. Alan Vickers turned away from them for a moment and, searching the office, spied a folded newspaper. He snatched it up and pounded it on the desk.

"Have you seen this? I don't mean the front page. Every-one of you'd turned sick at that. I mean, this piece here on the inside; the assassination of Wild Bill Hickok, two days ago, in Deadwood. You read about it, Captain?"

Captain Ash nodded. "His number was up."

"And who put it up? Who was the assassin? Do you re-member his name, after reading it here this morning? Did you ever hear the name before? No, of course not. Jack McCall. And who in the goddam hell is Jack McCall? A puling, insignificant, yellow-hearted amateur badman. He killed Wild Bill Hickok, as fancy a gun artist as ever put a bullet between a man's eyes. Wild Bill Hickok, shot in the back by man named Jack McCall. . . ."

Vickers' jaws clamped together and his eyes glittered as they came to focus on Captain Ash. "I want a man," he said grimly, "a dirty, cowardly skunk who'd shoot his best friend in the back. I want a man like that, Captain Ash; a man like Jack McCall. . . ."

Captain Ash's face became gray. "To assassinate Jim Chapman?"

"And how else is he going to be put out of the way? By a brave man walking up to him and telling him to go to his gun? Damn, no. Wild Bill Hickok was in Deadwood. He saw Chapman, and didn't cut himself in. . . . It's the only way, Ash. Do you know any other way—after last night?"

Captain Ash shook his head. "All right, I know the man. I have his name here in this book." He took a small note-book from his pocket. "Hob—one of my spies—dropped his name one time and I wrote it down. I looked him over and I believe he will do it. It'll take some persuasion, of course, but . . . his name is Andy Welker."

"Welker? A relation of Clark Welker?"

"His young brother. He's only twenty years old. He's got a yellow streak four inches wide running down his back. I could have arrested him, three months ago, when he held up a storekeeper over at Richmond. A man sixty-four years old. Welker laid open the old man's scalp and broke his nose. . . . I thought I'd save Welker—for an emergency."

"This is the emergency," said Alan Vickers. "Get the boy here. I'll persuade him. Wants to be like his older brother, does he? So he breaks an old man's nose. All right, he's the lad for us. I'll give him the razzle-dazzle. . . ."

Captain Ash came into the room where Alan Vickers was dozing in the swivel chair. He said, "Chief, this is Andy Welker."

Vickers swung his chair around and regarded the sullen youth in the patched flannel shirt and faded overalls. "So you're Clark Welker's brother?"

"You got nothin' on me," Andy Welker said defiantly. "You turn me loose or you'll get in trouble. You can't prove a thing on me."

"Why," said Alan Vickers, "has anyone told you they have anything against you? Did you, Captain Ash?"

"I think I could persuade a storekeeper over at Richmond to make an identification."

"Try it!" snarled Andy Welker. "Try it and see what it gets you. No one in Richmond finks on a Welker. Just because my brother got his doesn't mean folks aren't still plenty scared. . . ."

"Sure," said Alan Vickers. "Don't I know it? I tried for ten years to get something on the Chapman outfit and what'd they do to me in Clay and Ray Counties?"

"They laughed at you," said Andy Welker cockily. "They never snitched on Jim Chapman. No one ever did that. Not any that wanted to live."

"You're telling me!" Vickers exclaimed. "They got away with a million dollars—Jim Chapman and your brother and all the rest and I got the horse laugh. I suppose your family is pretty well fixed these days, eh, Welker?"

Andy Welker turned sullen again. "We get by."

Vickers nodded thoughtfully. "I don't doubt it. Clark must have salted away plenty. But . . . Andy, how would you like to make five thousand dollars?"

Andy Welker looked at Alan Vickers and snorted.

"As a matter of fact," Vickers went on, "five thousand isn't very much money. Ten thousand is a lot more. Ten thousand dollars. . . ."

Twenty-seven

THEY KNEW in Clay County. They knew that Vickers detectives had surrounded Ed Taylor's home by night and perforated it with more than a hundred bullet holes.

So Jim Chapman was back. After all these years . . . after Northport. So there were Vickers spies in the country, after all. But they had failed again, as they had always failed. Old Jim Chapman had scared the hell out of them. A dozen Vickers men—twenty—thirty; they had surrounded him in his sister's house and he had shot the hell out of them. As he always had.

And now—now he was in the brush, of course. The boys had always been in the brush.

They came looking for him. Not the Vickers men, but the old-timers and some who had grown up since, who knew the brush.

Chapman saw the first one when he woke up the second morning. It was Abe Colton, who had lost his right arm during the war.

He was hunkered on his heels on the ground, a few feet from where Chapman lay. "Hello, Jim," Colton said. "It's been a long time."

"Abe! You came up on me while I slept!"

Colton grinned. "S'all right. No Vickers men could do it. Anyway, they're gone. Lige Whickers followed their trail a little ways. . . . It ran past Hobson's place."

"I suppose so," Chapman said dully. "How many were there?"

"Tracks of eight or nine. Uh—what d'you think of Hobson?"

"What's the use? If it wouldn't be him, it'd be someone else."

A hundred feet away someone whistled twice; softly. Abe Colton half straightened, then hunkered down again. "Young Andy Welker."

"Welker." Chapman sat up.

Young Welker came up. He looked more like Clarence than Clark and he was no more than twenty.

"Hello, Mr. Chapman," he said, "I'm Clark's brother. . . ."

"I'm sorry, Andy. I thought a lot of Clark."

"I know. Oh, sure, I know. Clark had tough luck—"

"What?" exclaimed Chapman.

"Well," said young Andy Welker. "If a man's got to die that's as good as any way. Fighting like hell, taking along a sheriff or—"

"You fool!" snarled Chapman, "what are you talking about? Do you think Clark enjoyed the kind of life he led? Go back to your home—your school."

Andy Welker blinked in astonishment. He backed away, his eyes slitting admiringly. Yes, this Jim Chapman was a honey. Tougher even than they said he was.

Abe Colton said, "What brought you, Andy?"

"Oh—I almost forgot. Message for Mr. Chapman. Ed—I mean Mr. Taylor, sent it. He knew that I know this brush like a book and—"

"The message," Chapman snarled.

The boy flushed. "Why he just told me to tell you that Evel . . . I mean he said, just to tell you that *she* wants to see you. Said you'd know. . . ."

"All right, I know."

Chapman got up and young Welker faded into the brush. Colton said, "I brought you a bite of breakfast."

"Thanks, Abe."

He munched the food, then suddenly he said, "How is she, Abe?"

"Fine," Abe said. "Fine . . . I guess. Her father passed on five-six years ago. Cliff runs the bank. He never married." Abe rubbed his whiskered jaw with his one hand and looked sharply at Chapman. Then he said, "You know about Halliday bein' the prosecuting attorney of the county?"

"I think I heard something about it. Well, Abe, thanks for everything."

Colton took the dismissal and went off silently. Chapman waited a while, then started off in the opposite direction.

He came out of the woods within ten feet of where he had come out ten years ago, after the bullet of the ruffian Pike had brought him down. He remembered how he had seen her working in her garden, wearing a gingham dress and a sunbonnet.

She wasn't in the garden today. In fact, there was no garden. Waist high weeds grew where the garden once had been. A Negro was splitting wood in the back yard. He saw Chapman but did not miss a stroke of his axe.

Chapman crossed the patch of weeds and moved toward

the white pillared veranda. He was ten feet from it when the
door opened and Martin Halliday stepped out.

Halliday's face paled. "You!" he exclaimed.

There was a rustle in the door behind him and Evelyn appeared.

Chapman said, "Hello."

That he would have to see her after all these years, when
Halliday was beside her. He said to Halliday, "Don't go.
I was just—passing."

He could see that Halliday was perspiring freely and it gave
him small pleasure. The prosecuting attorney of the county
facing the most desperate criminal the country had ever
known—and nothing he could do about it. Nothing, at least
that would help him in the fulfillment of his sworn public
duty. Other things. . . .

Evelyn said, "Come inside, Jim."

Chapman advanced and Halliday gave way for him. Chapman smiled crookedly. "After you, Halliday."

That was what they expected, wasn't it? He, the hunted
man who allowed no one to get behind his back. Yes, she'd
wanted to see him, but when he'd come her lover was with
her. Naturally, Chapman couldn't trust him to leave. Halliday
was a rival—and the county prosecutor.

He was shaking, even.

Chapman came abreast of him and stretched out his arm
to herd him ahead. Then Evelyn stopped it.

"You'd better go, Martin."

The flame was burning at white heat, now. It seared and it
made Chapman continue. "Why, I don't think I can let you
go, Halliday."

But he let his arm drop and stepped past Halliday, following
Evelyn into the house. He did not look back at Halliday.
The prosecutor was not a shooting man and—there was
Evelyn.

They faced each other, then, after nine years. It was Evelyn
who spoke first. "I wanted to see you, Jim."

His eyes bored into hers. They were not sad and they were
not glad. They were—empty. Chapman seemed empty, he felt
all hollow inside. The cheap little scene with Halliday outside
had failed to bolster him.

She was waiting for him to speak and he had no words. A
faint pink came to her smooth cheeks.

She had not changed, had scarcely aged.

His silence forced her to say, "Well, Jim?"

His lips parted. "Why, I'm Jim Chapman. . . ."

The cheeks were red now, the eyes narrower at the corners. "Why did you come back?"

"Because . . ." He laughed shortly, but there was no humor in it. "Because . . ." Where were the words? "I don't know. There are still places I haven't seen."

"You're lying, Jim. You've seen them all. And they've all been the same. Black. You never saw the places you went, you never wanted to see them."

"All right," he said, "and you?"

She stiffened a little and the color receded to her throat. "Martin Halliday . . ."

She couldn't say the rest of it, but there wasn't any reason to say it. He knew. He had always known. Martin had waited ten years.

He nodded. "You should have done it long ago. I—expected it."

He knew of course that she hadn't done it until she could tell him first. She was that way and he hadn't been here in all these years. So she had waited.

He half turned away. "Halliday's all right. Be a big man some day."

"Yes," she agreed.

Where was Alan Vickers now? In Kansas City? Firing the cravens who had had Jim Chapman surrounded and then discovered that they couldn't do it after all? Old Alan—yes, he had gotten old, chasing Chapman—would give them what they lacked. He'd give them the steel they needed in their arms.

Some time.

The door was four feet from Chapman and he could not move toward it. He wanted more than he had ever wanted anything in the world, to pass through that door . . . and he couldn't. A fine moisture filmed his forehead. He knew now what he had to do.

Why didn't she say the word that would loosen his feet from the floor?

They were finished with their talk. She had said what she had wanted to say and he had made the answers. There was no more.

Outside, a stick of wood flew from under Rupe's axe and hit the back of the house with a thud. The noise broke the spell and released Chapman.

He stepped to the door, saying, "The best, of course, Evelyn," and he pushed against the screen. He pushed it out a foot and let it come back on its spring.

". . . woman in Deadwood?" Evelyn was saying.

He turned. His sister had asked him that, and he had told her, "She was someone I met years ago." He told Evelyn the same thing and even as he spoke the words, it crashed against him with stunning force.

Why should Evelyn ask about Vivian Morgan?

Gasping, he stared at her.

"I have a right to know. I have a right to know *from you*. They said she was your friend."

"She was my friend," he said, wondering. "She was my friend and she tried to help. . . ."

"She didn't try," Evelyn said fiercely. "I read the papers, I read between the lines. She didn't *try* to help you. She *did*. She died for you and *what right did she have to die for you?*"

For the first time in years he floundered. Why had Vivian Morgan died for him? Because she loved him? Of course, but why should Evelyn . . .

"I said, what right did she have to die for you?" Evelyn repeated. "I am your wife and I didn't die for you?"

Bewildered, he shook his head. "I . . . I . . . don't—"

She cut him off. "She only loved you. She wasn't your wife. She had no right to die for you. I had the right . . . and I ran away. I was the coward and I lived nine years. I let her die. . . ."

"Evelyn!" he cried hoarsely.

Deliberately, fiercely, she walked toward him and even then he stared, stupidly. She stood up on her toes and put her arms about him and his went automatically about her. He felt her body, hot against his.

The flame blazed up and wiped away everything in a terrifying holocaust, and still . . . it survived. In the eternity he stood there he knew that it couldn't be.

The road didn't go back. It went straight ahead and it was a short road. The hill was just ahead and he was riding toward it on the swiftest horse in the world.

He pushed her away and she whispered. "I was too young, Jim. It hurt too much, but it doesn't hurt now. It won't. That woman showed me how. I'll go with you."

Dully he said, "You can't. Not any more. Alan Vickers is closing in—"

"Not on you!" she cried. "You're Jim Chapman. You've made a fool of Alan Vickers and all his men for ten years. I've watched you do it—over and over, and over. You only have to do it once more. This time we'll lose them for good.

We'll go to Europe. South America. We can live any-where. . . ."

The loop was that big. No one knew better than Jim Chapman just how big it was. He was Jim Chapman on the Pampas, in the Never-Never land of Australia. Wherever man's foot had set, he was Jim Chapman.

He had been a legend before Northport. The legend became alive at Northport.

"All right," he said suddenly. "We'll try it. Europe. I've never been in Europe."

He lied. He was in Europe. Once Clem Tancred had brought him a newspaper clipping, which told about a Russian outlaw who had been killed by Cossacks. "The Jim Chap-man of the Volga," the clipping had said.

"I've got some things to get," he went on.

"No. You don't need anything. I don't want you to go, with-out me. I'm ready now. . . ."

He smiled at her gently. "But you can't go like that. Pack a bag. I've got to see Ed and my sister. Something that can't wait. . . ."

Her eyes clouded. "How long will it take?"

"An hour. Not more than an hour and a half. I'll be back before you're packed and then—Europe!"

"I'll be ready. I'll be waiting. . . ."

He kissed her—briefly, so she wouldn't suspect, then smiling, stepped out. He did not hear her whisper, "Jim . . . I'm afraid! . . ."

"I'll be waiting. . . ."

Yes, she would wait. As long as Jim Chapman was alive, she would wait. She would go with him, too. Anywhere that he went, for she was his wife.

Chapman walked back through the patch of weeds that had once been her garden. There was a ringing in his ears. He walked as he had not walked in many years, a loose-limbed, swinging stride. The walk of a man who was *alive*.

He had won.

Clem Tancred, Hutch, Ed; the others—they had lived and died and had never known it.

Chapman had won. He knew now. . . .

And he could walk away.

She would wait . . . until he was gone. She owed him that because he had been so alone, all of his life, because he had been like a hunted beast, because . . .

He had won and so now he could ride up the road, he

could put the spurs to his horse and gallop it to the crest.

From the brush, young Andy Welker called to him.

"Mr. Chapman."

Chapman saw the boy and smiled. "Hello, Andy. You followed me? Takes a good woodsman to do that."

"Well, I was raised in the brush. Uh, Mr. Chapman . . . everything all right—over there, I mean?"

"Yes, Andy. Thanks for bringing me the message."

"Oh, that's all right, Mr. Chapman. . . . Uh, mind if I walk along with you—a little ways?"

"The brush is free, Andy. I don't own it. Come along."

Andy Welker fell in beside Jim Chapman. After a little way he fell a step behind. . . .